Dracula
吸血鬼德古拉

Original Author   Bram Stoker
Adaptor   Brian J. Stuart
Illustrator   Julina Alekcangra

WORDS
1000

MP3

Let's Enjoy Masterpieces!

All the beautiful fairy tales and masterpieces that you have encountered during your childhood remain as warm memories in your adulthood. This time, let's indulge in the world of masterpieces through English. You can enjoy the depth and beauty of original works, which you can't enjoy through Chinese translations.

The stories are easy for you to understand because of your familiarity with them. When you enjoy reading, your ability to understand English will also rapidly improve.

This series of *Let's Enjoy Masterpieces* is a special reading comprehension booster program, devised to improve reading comprehension for beginners whose command of English is not satisfactory, or who are elementary, middle, and high school students. With this program, you can enjoy reading masterpieces in English with fun and efficiency.

This carefully planned program is composed of 5 levels, from the beginner level of 350 words to the intermediate and advanced levels of 1,000 words. With this program's level-by-level system, you are able to read famous texts in English and to savor the true pleasure of the world's language.

The program is well conceived, composed of reader-friendly explanations of English expressions and grammar, quizzes to help the student learn vocabulary and understand the meaning of the texts, and fabulous illustrations that adorn every page. In addition, with our "Guide to Listening," not only is reading comprehension enhanced but also listening comprehension skills are highlighted.

In the audio recording of the book, texts are vividly read by professional American actors. The texts are rewritten, according to the levels of the readers by an expert editorial staff of native speakers, on the basis of standard American English with the ministry of education recommended vocabulary. Therefore, it will be of great help even for all the students that want to learn English.

Please indulge yourself in the fun of reading and listening to English through *Let's Enjoy Masterpieces*.

伯蘭 • 史杜克 Bram Stoker (1847~1912)

Bram Stoker was born on November 8, 1847, in Dublin, Ireland. During his childhood he was physically weak and often bedridden. He loved reading and writing in his youth, and he wanted to become a writer someday despite his father's intense opposition. After graduating from Trinity College, he became a civil servant.

While in the civil service, Stoker used every spare moment to work as a drama critic and a magazine editor. Soon he met Henry Irving, an actor with whom he established a lifelong friendship. This association seemed to have a great influence on Stoker's entire career.

In 1878 Bram Stoker married Florence Balcombe, whose former suitor was Oscar Wilde, a writer, poet, and drama critic. Stoker then left his civil service job of eight years and moved to London, where he worked as the manager of the Lyceum Theater, which Henry Irving owned.

Stoker faithfully fulfilled his job duties and also worked as a writer. In addition to his first published work, *Duties of Clerks of Petty Sessions in Ireland*, which was published in 1879, many more of his long and short stories were published. In 1897, Stoker's Gothic horror novel *Dracula* won his worldwide fame. He was a genuine, tireless writer who devoted himself to writing until his death on April 20, 1912.

Dracula

The story begins with the Englishman Jonathan Harker heading to meet Count Dracula, who lives in an old castle in Transylvania, Romania. Harker is easy prey to the temptations of Count Dracula, who tricks Harker under the pretense of purchasing a house in London.

Dracula is really a vampire, who exists only by drinking the blood of living people. The vampire has lived for several centuries in his castle with three female vampires. Throughout his stay in the castle, Harker is seized with fear and suspicion. As he becomes aware that he is being held captive by Dracula, Harker takes decisive action at the risk of his own life to escape from the vampire's castle.

Meanwhile, Harker's fiancee, Mina, lives together with her friend Lucy. Lucy suddenly starts going outside their home at night. Mina becomes worried about Lucy turning paler and paler every day as her strange behavior continues . . .

Dracula, a masterpiece of Bram Stoker, has been performed on the stage and made into movies hundreds of times. It always gives audiences sensations of thrill and horror and sometimes causes them to stay awake all night as they confront their fears.

HOW TO USE THIS BOOK

本書使用說明

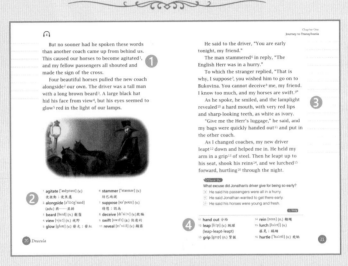

1 *Original English texts*

It is easy to understand the meaning of the text, because the text is rewritten according to the levels of the readers.

2 *Explanation of the vocabulary*

The words and expressions that include vocabulary above the elementary level are clearly defined.

3 *Response notes*

Spaces are included in the book so you can take notes about what you don't understand or what you want to remember.

4 *Check UP*

Review quizzes to check your understanding of the text.

🎧 *Audio Recording*

In the audio recording, native speakers narrate the texts in standard American English. By combining the written words and the audio recording, you can listen to English with great ease.

Audio books have been popular in Britain and America for many decades. They allow the listener to experience the proper word pronunciation and sentence intonation that add important meaning and drama to spoken English. Students will benefit from listening to the recording twenty or more times.

After you are familiar with the text and recording, listen once more with your eyes closed to check your listening comprehension. Finally, after you can listen with your eyes closed and understand every word and every sentence, you are then ready to mimic the native speaker.

Then you should make a recording by reading the text yourself. Then play both recordings to compare your oral skills with those of a native speaker.

HOW TO IMPROVE READING ABILITY

如何增進英文閱讀能力

1 Catch key words

Read the key words in the sentences and practice catching the gist of the meaning of the sentence. You might question how working with a few important words could enhance your reading ability. However, it's quite effective. If you continue to use this method, you will find out that the key words and your knowledge of people and situations enables you to understand the sentence.

2 Divide long sentences

Read in chunks of meaning, dividing sentences into meaningful chunks of information. In the book, chunks are arranged in sentences according to meaning. If you consider the sentences backwards or grammatically, your reading speed will be slow and you will find it difficult to listen to English.

You are ready to move to a more sophisticated level of comprehension when you find that narrowly focusing on chunks is irritating. Instead of considering the chunks, you will make it a habit to read the sentence from the beginning to the end to figure out the meaning of the whole.

③ Make inferences and assumptions

Making inferences and assumptions is part of your ability. If you don't know, try to guess the meaning of the words. Although you don't know all the words in context, don't go straight to the dictionary. Developing an ability to make inferences in the context is important.

The first way to figure out the meaning of a word is from its context. If you cannot make head or tail out of the meaning of a word, look at what comes before or after it. Ask yourself what can happen in such a situation. Make your best guess as to the word's meaning. Then check the explanations of the word in the book or look up the word in a dictionary.

④ Read a lot and reread the same book many times

There is no shortcut to mastering English. Only if you do a lot of reading will you make your way to the summit. Read fun and easy books with an average of less than one new word per page. Try to immerse yourself in English as often as you can.

Spend time "swimming" in English. Language learning research has shown that immersing yourself in English will help you improve your English, even though you may not be aware of what you're learning.

CONTENTS

Before You Read

Dracula

For centuries[1], I have lived in the dark in my Transylvania castle[2]. The villagers[3] all around know me and fear me. It's time to travel to a new land where the people do not know me. Therefore, I have sent for[4] a young real estate[5] lawyer[6] from London. He will help me prepare to move there, but he will never leave my castle! Haha!

Jonathan Harker

I am a young lawyer in the real estate business. My boss has sent me to Transylvania to serve a very wealthy client named Count[7] Dracula. This count wants to buy a property[8] in London, and he has very specific needs. I must leave my beautiful fiancee[9], Mina, to attend to[10] this business. When I return after several weeks, we will get married.

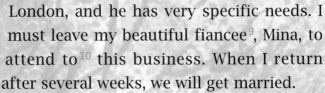

1. century ['sɛntʃəri] (n.) 世紀
2. castle ['kæsəl] (n.) 城堡
3. villager ['vɪlɪdʒər] (n.) 村民
4. send for 派人去叫
5. real estate 房地產
6. lawyer ['lɔːjər] (n.) 律師
7. count [kaʊnt] (n.) 伯爵
8. property ['prɑːpərti] (n.) 財產

Mina

My darling[11] Jonathan has been called away[12] on business to a strange country I have never heard of. I do hope he will be safe! When he returns, we will marry! For now, I will help my best friend, Lucy, prepare for her own wedding to a nice English gentleman.

Arthur Holmwood

I am a wealthy English gentleman who has an estate[13] in London. I am to[14] be married soon, to a beautiful young lady named[15] Lucy. However, she has fallen seriously ill. I would do anything to help her!

Van Helsing

I am a professor[16] and doctor who lives in Amsterdam. I specialize in[17] strange illnesses. One of my former students, Dr. John Seward has called me to London to help care for a sick young woman. I wonder what has happened to this young lady.

---

9. **fiancee** [ˌfiːɑːnˈseɪ] (n.) 未婚妻
10. **attend to** 關心；注意
11. **darling** [ˈdɑːrlɪŋ] (a.) 親愛的
12. **call away** 叫走
13. **estate** [ɪˈsteɪt] (n.) 資產
14. **be + to** 即將
15. **name** [neɪm] (v.) 名為；叫做
16. **professor** [prəˈfesər] (n.) 教授
17. **specialize in** 專攻

Chapter One

Journey¹ to Transylvania

I n early 1897, the London lawyer² Jonathan Harker traveled from London to Transylvania to meet a client³ named Count Dracula. Harker worked in real estate⁴; the count wanted to buy some property⁵ in London. This is Harker's journal⁶:

3 May

Count Dracula told me to stay at the Golden Krone Hotel in Bistritz. This is a scenic⁷ town in the shadow of the Carpathian Mountains. As soon as I arrived, the innkeeper's⁸ wife gave me a letter.

---

1. **journey** [ˈdʒɜːrni] (n.) 旅程
2. **lawyer** [ˈlɔːjər] (n.) 律師
3. **client** [ˈklaɪənt] (n.) 客戶
4. **real estate** 房地產
5. **property** [ˈprɑːpərti] (n.) 房產
6. **journal** [ˈdʒɜːrnəl] (n.) 日誌
7. **scenic** [ˈsiːnɪk] (a.) 風景秀麗的
8. **innkeeper** [ˈɪnˌkiːpər] (n.) 旅館主人
9. **coach** [koʊtʃ] (n.) 馬車

It read,

My Friend,

Welcome to the Carpathians. Sleep well tonight. At three tomorrow afternoon, a coach[9] will leave for the town of Bukovina. I have reserved[10] a seat for you. When you get to Borgo Pass, you will meet my driver, who will bring you to me.

Your friend,
Dracula

4 May

When I asked the innkeeper about the Count, he acted strangely. Before, he understood my basic German well. But when I asked about Dracula, he told me he didn't understand. He and his wife gave each other frightened[11] looks. Finally, after I kept asking[12], they told me that they knew nothing. Then they made the sign[13] of the cross. This was all very odd[14].

---

10. **reserve** [rɪˈzɜːrv] (v.) 預約
11. **frightened** [ˈfraɪtnd] (a.) 驚恐的

12. **keep V-ing** 持續地做某事
13. **sign** [saɪn] (n.) 手勢；符號
14. **odd** [ɑːd] (a.) 詭異的

Just as I had finished packing[1] my suitcase for the trip, the old lady nervously came into my room.

"Young Herr[2], do you really have to go?" she asked.

I replied I had to go, as it was business. She asked me if I really knew where and what I was going to do. Finally, she got on her knees and begged me not to go.

"What silliness[3]," I thought. I helped her stand up and told her firmly[4] that it was my business to go, and nothing could interfere[5] with that. She wiped[6] tears from her eyes. Then she took off the crucifix[7] that hung around her neck and put it around my neck.

"For your mother's sake[8]," she said before leaving my room.

1. **pack** [pæk] (v.) 打包
2. **Herr** [hɛːr] (n.)
   【德】先生；德國紳士
3. **silliness** [ˈsɪlɪnɪs] (n.) 愚蠢
4. **firmly** [ˈfɜːrmli] (adv.)
   堅定地
5. **interfere** [ˌɪntərˈfɪr] (v.)
   妨礙；干涉

I am writing this as I wait for the coach. There are many townspeople[9] around the inn talking about me. I looked up in my dictionary the few words I could catch. If I am right, these words are "*Ordog*," which means Satan[10], and "*vrolok*," which means something that is either wolf or vampire[11]. These are quaint[12] superstitions[13].

Here comes the coach now. Better late than never!

6. **wipe** [waɪp] (v.) 擦拭

7. **crucifix** [ˈkruːsɪfɪks] (n.) 十字架

8. **for one's sake** 為了某緣故

9. **townspeople** [ˈtaʊnzpiːpəl] (n.) 鎮民

10. **Satan** [ˈseɪtn] (n.) 撒旦魔鬼

11. **vampire** [ˈvæmpaɪr] (n.) 吸血鬼

12. **quaint** [kweɪnt] (a.) 古怪的

13. **superstition** [ˌsuːpərˈstɪʃən] (n.) 迷信

🎧 **3**   *5 May*

I am at Count Dracula's castle[1] now.
The journey took many hours, and it was a
strange one.

We soon left the inn behind and entered a
wild and beautiful countryside. Before us lay a
green sloping[2] land full of forests and woods,
with steep[3] hills to the right and left.
The afternoon sun brought out all the
glorious[4] colors of this beautiful range.

---

1. **castle** [ˈkæsəl] (n.) 城堡
2. **sloping** [ˈsloʊpɪŋ] (a.)
   有坡度的
3. **steep** [stiːp] (a.) 陡峭的
4. **glorious** [ˈglɔːriəs] (a.)
   壯麗的；極好的

5. **sink** [sɪŋk] (v.) 沉沒
6. **passenger** [ˈpæsɪndʒər]
   (n.) 乘客
7. **urge** [ɜːrdʒ] (v.) 催促
8. **lash** [læʃ] (v.) 鞭打

Soon the sun sank[5] low behind us. At dark, the passengers[6] became excited, and it seemed they were urging[7] the driver to go faster. He lashed[8] the horses unmercifully[9] with his long whip[10] to pick up their speed[11]. Then the mountains closed in on either side. We were entering the Borgo Pass.

It was obvious[12] that something very exciting was expected, but though I asked each passenger, no one would give me the slightest[13] explanation[14]. I was looking for a driver who would take me to the Count. I expected to see lamps through the blackness[15], but all was dark.

I was thinking about what I was going to do when the driver, looking at his watch, said, "There is no coach waiting for you here. Perhaps the Count does not expect you after all[16]. You should come on to Bukovina and return tomorrow or the next day, or even better, the day after that."

---

9. **unmercifully**
   [ʌnˈmɜːrsɪfəli] (adv.)
   冷酷地；無情地
10. **whip** [wɪp] (n.) 鞭子
11. **pick up one's speed** 加速
12. **obvious** [ˈɑːbviəs] (a.)
   明顯的

13. **slightest** [ˈslaɪtɪst] (a.)
   最不重要的
14. **explanation**
   [ˌekspləˈneɪʃən] (n.) 解釋
15. **blackness** [ˈblæknɪs]
   (n.) 黑暗
16. **after all** 到底；結果

19

But no sooner had he spoken these words than another coach came up from behind us. This caused our horses to become agitated[1], and my fellow passengers all shouted and made the sign of the cross.

Four beautiful horses pulled the new coach alongside[2] our own. The driver was a tall man with a long brown beard[3]. A large black hat hid his face from view[4], but his eyes seemed to glow[5] red in the light of our lamps.

1. **agitate** [ˈædʒɪteɪt] (v.)
   使激動;使焦慮
2. **alongside** [əˈlɔːŋˈsaɪd]
   (adv.) 與……並排
3. **beard** [bɪrd] (n.) 鬍鬚
4. **view** [vjuː] (n.) 視野
5. **glow** [gloʊ] (v.) 發光;發紅

6. **stammer** [ˈstæmər] (v.)
   結巴地說
7. **suppose** [səˈpoʊz] (v.)
   猜想;認為
8. **deceive** [dɪˈsiːv] (v.)欺騙
9. **swift** [swɪft] (a.) 快速的
10. **reveal** [rɪˈviːl] (v.) 顯露

He said to the driver, "You are early tonight, my friend."

The man stammered[6] in reply, "The English Herr was in a hurry."

To which the stranger replied, "That is why, I suppose[7], you wished him to go on to Bukovina. You cannot deceive[8] me, my friend. I know too much, and my horses are swift.[9]"

As he spoke, he smiled, and the lamplight revealed[10] a hard mouth, with very red lips and sharp-looking teeth, as white as ivory.

"Give me the Herr's luggage," he said, and my bags were quickly handed out[11] and put in the other coach.

As I changed coaches, my new driver leapt[12] down and helped me in. He held my arm in a grip[13] of steel. Then he leapt up to his seat, shook his reins[14], and we lurched[15] forward, hurtling[16] through the night.

✓ *Check Up*

What excuse did Jonathan's driver give for being so early?

- a　He said his passengers were all in a hurry.
- b　He said Jonathan wanted to get there early.
- c　He said his horses were young and fresh.

Ans: b

---

11. **hand out** 分給
12. **leap** [liːp] (v.) 跳躍
    (leap-leapt-leapt)
13. **grip** [grɪp] (n.) 緊握
14. **rein** [reɪn] (n.) 韁繩
15. **lurch** [lɜːrtʃ] (v.)
    搖晃；蹣跚
16. **hurtle** [ˈhɜːrtl] (v.) 飛馳

21

This is where my journey became even stranger. At first, I thought we were going around in a circle. I fixed my eyes[1] on the top of a mountain where it met the sky, and realized that we were indeed making a large circle around the pass. By this time, we were near the far side of the pass.

I do not recall[2] falling asleep, but I must have. It seemed like we traveled a long way before the coach suddenly stopped. I snapped[3] to my senses[4] and saw that we were in the courtyard[5] of an ancient, crumbling[6] castle, and were before a huge wooden door.

The driver was already on the ground with my luggage. He helped me out with the same iron[7] grip as before. Then he jumped up without a word, shook the reins, turned the coach around and disappeared.

As I stood there alone wondering what to do, many questions filled my head. What sort of place had I come to? What sort of grim[8] adventure was I on?

---

1. **fix one's eyes** 注視
2. **recall** [rɪ'kɔːl] (v.) 記得
3. **snap** [snæp] (v.) 突然做 (snap-snapped-snapped)
4. **senses** ['sensɪs] (n.) 〔複〕知覺
5. **courtyard** ['kɔːrtjɑːrd] (n.) 庭院
6. **crumble** ['krʌmbəl] (v.) 摧毀；碎裂
7. **iron** ['aɪrn] (a.) 剛強的
8. **grim** [grɪm] (a.) 恐怖陰森的

These questions were interrupted by the sound of the great door opening. There stood an old man, clean shaven[9] except for a long mustache[10], dressed all in black and holding a lamp.

There was not a drop of color anywhere about him, even in his pale, white face. He motioned[11] to me very formally with his right hand. His English was excellent, but he spoke with a strange intonation[12].

Which is not true about the Count's appearance?

a He looks very tall and muscular.

b His clothes are completely black.

c He is very formal and speaks English well.

Ans: a

---

9. **clean shaven**
   鬍子刮得很乾淨
10. **mustache** [ˈmʌstæʃ] (n.)
    小鬍子
11. **motion** [ˈmouʃən] (v.)
    打手勢
12. **intonation** [ˌɪntəˈneɪʃən]
    (n.) 語調;聲調

23

"Welcome to my house! Enter freely and of your own free will[1]!"

The instant that I had stepped over the threshold[2], he grasped my hand with his, which felt more dead than alive. However, it possessed[3] the same unnatural strength as that of the driver. I was so surprised that for a minute, I thought that he was the driver. To make sure, I suddenly said, "Count Dracula?"

1. **will** [wɪl] (n.) 意願
2. **threshold** [ˈθreʃoʊld] (n.) 門檻
3. **possess** [pəˈzes] (v.) 擁有
4. **bow** [baʊ] (v.) 鞠躬；欠身
5. **bid (bid-bade-bidden)** [bɪd] (v.) 向……表示
6. **available** [əˈveɪləbəl] (a.) 有空的

He bowed[4] formally as he replied, "I am Dracula, and I bid[5] you welcome, Mr. Harker, to my house. Come in. You must need to eat and rest."

He carried my bags along the passage, saying it was late, so no servants were available[6]. We went up a great winding[7] stair and along a great passage[8]. At the end of this, he threw open a heavy door, and I rejoiced[9] to see within a well-lit[10] dining room. In the large fireplace, a bright, hot fire flared[11].

The Count opened another door, which led into a great bedroom warmed with another log[12] fire. The Count left my luggage inside and said, "When you are ready, you will find your supper prepared in the dining room."

Check Up Short answer question.
What did the Count's strength make Jonathan think?

_____

Ans: He thought the Count was the driver.

7. **winding** [ˈwaɪndɪŋ] (a.) 曲折的
8. **passage** [ˈpæsɪdʒ] (n.) 通道
9. **rejoice** [rɪˈdʒɔɪs] (v.) 高興

10. **well-lit** [ˈwelɪt] (a.) 明亮的
11. **flare** [fler] (v.) 燃燒
12. **log** [lɑːg] (n.) 原木；木材

🎧 7

All my doubts and fears vanished[1]. I realized that I was starving[2]. After washing up quickly, I went to eat. My host[3] made a graceful wave to the table, and said, "Please enjoy your dinner. Excuse the fact that I have already eaten."

After dinner, we sat together by the fire. I studied him closely, for he had many strange features[4]. His face was strong and long, and he had a high, thin nose. His forehead was high and domed[5], and his thick white hair was tightly pulled back. The Count's eyebrows[6] were very thick and almost met in the middle.

His mouth looked cruel, even when he smiled. I could see two of his white teeth, which protruded[7] out over his surprisingly red lips. The teeth were strangely pointed. In contrast to[8] his lips, the rest of his face was quite white.

---

1. **vanish** ['vænɪʃ] (v.) 消失
2. **starve** [stɑːrv] (v.) 飢餓
3. **host** [hoʊst] (n.) 主人
4. **feature** ['fiːtʃər] (n.) 特徵
5. **domed** [doʊmd] (a.) 半球形的
6. **eyebrow** ['aɪbraʊ] (n.) 眉毛
7. **protrude** [proʊ'truːd] (v.) 突出；伸出
8. **in contrast to** 相較於
9. **broad** [brɔːd] (a.) 寬的
10. **pointed** ['pɔɪntɪd] (a.) 尖的
11. **lean** [liːn] (v.) 傾身；屈身
12. **decay** [dɪ'keɪ] (n.) 腐爛
13. **nauseate** ['nɑːzieɪt] (v.) 作嘔；厭惡
14. **reaction** [ri'ækʃən] (n.) 反應

His fingers were short and broad[9], and they had long pointed[10] fingernails. When he leaned[11] close to me, I could smell a sort of decay[12] on this breath. This nauseated[13] me, and the Count drew back after seeing my reaction[14].

"You must be tired," he said. "Your bedroom is all ready, and tomorrow you may sleep as late as you want. I have to be away till the afternoon, so sleep well, and dream well!"

✓ *Check Up* True or False.

a. The Count's teeth were yellow and chipped. ____
b. The Count's breath smelled rotten. ____
c. Jonathan and the Count had a big dinner together. ____

Ans: a F b T c F

7 May

After my late breakfast the next day, I met the Count in the library. There were many English books there. I asked if I could visit the library whenever I wanted.

He answered, "Certainly." And he added, "You may go anywhere in the castle, except where the doors are locked. We are in Transylvania, and Transylvania is not England. Our ways are not your ways, and you may find many things strange here."

This led to much conversation. Finally, our conversation turned to our business.

"Come," he said, "tell me of London and the house you have prepared for me."

I produced[1] the real estate papers for a large estate named Carfax. The Count had sent a description[2] of what he desired, and Carfax was a good match[3]. It was an old house that

---

1. **produce** [prə'duːs] (v.) 出示；拿出
2. **description** [dɪ'skrɪpʃən] (n.) 描述
3. **match** [mætʃ] (n.) 符合
4. **Middle Ages** 中古世紀
5. **envelope** ['envəloʊp] (n.) 信封
6. **hidden** ['hɪdn] (a.) 隱密的
7. **jump to one's feet** 跳起來
8. **stay up** 熬夜
9. **courtly** ['kɔːrtli] (a.) 優雅的

had been built in the Middle Ages[4] and had been added to since. One part of it looked like a small castle, with thick walls and heavy doors. I had him sign the necessary papers and then put them in an envelope[5] with a letter I wrote to my boss.

When I had finished, he said, "I am glad that it is old and big. My family is old, and to live in a new house would kill me. An old house has many dark, hidden[6] places, and I love the shadows."

We talked some more, mostly about England. Suddenly, the Count jumped to his feet[7] and said, "Why, it is morning already! It's terrible of me to make you stay up[8] so long. You must make your conversation less interesting so that I may not forget how time flies."

With a courtly[9] bow, he quickly left me.

One Point Lesson

It's terrible of me to make you stay up so long.
我真不像話，讓你都不能睡了。

It's . . . of A + to 某事：A 去做某事是很 + 形容詞（kind, clever）。

e.g. It's foolish of you to make such a mistake.
你犯下這樣的錯是很不應該的。

Vlad becomes Count Dracula

Bram Stoker made Dracula famous the world over, but not many people have heard of Vlad Tepes. This 15th century prince was Stoker's inspiration[1] for the evil[2] Count Dracula.

Vlad Tepes was a prince of Wallachia, a Romanian land near Transylvania. He did not lead a very happy life. He was kidnapped[3] by the Turks and held hostage[4] for many years.

While he was in Istanbul, he got news that his father and older brother were killed by the nobles[5] of a neighboring region. When he was 17 years old, he led a force of Turks to retake[6] the throne[7] of Wallachia for himself.

1. inspiration [ˌɪnspɪˈreɪʃən] (n.) 靈感
2. evil [ˈiːvəl] (a.) 邪惡的
3. kidnap [ˈkɪdnæp] (v.) 綁架
4. hostage [ˈhɑːstɪdʒ] (n.) 人質
5. noble [ˈnoʊbəl] (n.) 貴族
6. retake [ˌriːˈteɪk] (v.) 取回
7. throne [θroʊn] (n.) 王位；王座

After he was successful, he got his terrible revenge[8] on the nobles who had killed his father and brother. He impaled[9] the old ones on long, sharp sticks. He then made the younger nobles and their families march to another town and build a castle[10] there. The work was hard and many died, but at last, they built Castle Dracula.

During his rule, Vlad killed thousands of his enemies by impaling them on sticks. This is how he earned the nickname "Vlad the Impaler[11]". It is also probably where Stoker got the idea that the only way to kill Dracula was to impale his heart with a wooden stake[12].

8. **revenge** [rɪˈvendʒ] (n.) 報復
9. **impale** [ɪmˈpeɪl] (v.) 刺穿
10. **castle** [ˈkæsəl] (n.) 城堡
11. **impaler** [ɪmˈpeɪlər] (n.) 刺穿者
12. **stake** [steɪk] (n.) 椿；棍

Chapter Two

Prisoner[1] in Castle Dracula

8 May

I am beginning to feel that there is something very strange about this place. I need to write only facts in my diary to control my imagination.

When I got up after a few hours of sleep, I started to shave[2]. My shaving glass hung by the window. Suddenly, I felt a hand on my shoulder, and I heard the Count's voice saying to me, "Good morning."

---

1. **prisoner** ['prɪzənər] (n.) 囚犯
2. **shave** [ʃeɪv] (v.) 刮鬍子
3. **slightly** ['slaɪtli] (adv.) 輕微地
4. **reflection** [rɪ'flekʃən] (n.) 映像
5. **blaze** [bleɪz] (v.) 顯示

6. **fury** ['fjʊri] (n.) 狂怒；暴怒
7. **grab** [græb] (v.) 抓
8. **back up** 退後
9. **string** [strɪŋ] (n.) 線；串繩
10. **bead** [biːd] (n.) 小珠子
11. **pass** [pæs] (v.) 消逝
12. **seize** [siːz] (v.) 沒收；扣押
13. **nothing but** 只有

I was greatly surprised that I had not seen him in the mirror. I jumped and cut myself slightly[3]. There was still no reflection[4] of the Count in my mirror even though he was just over my right shoulder!

Then I saw the cut and the blood on my chin. I turned, and when the Count saw my face, his eyes blazed[5] with fury[6]. He suddenly grabbed[7] for my throat. I backed up[8] and his hand touched the string[9] of beads[10] which held the crucifix. It made an instant change in him. The fury passed[11] so quickly that I could hardly believe it was ever there.

"Take care," he said, "how you cut yourself. It is more dangerous than you think in this country." Then seizing[12] the mirror, he added, "This is nothing but[13] trouble. Away with it!"

He wrenched open[1] the window with his terrible hand and he flung out[2] the mirror. It shattered[3] into a thousand pieces on the stones of the courtyard far below. Then he left without a word.

When I went into the dining room, breakfast was prepared, but I could not find the Count anywhere. So I breakfasted alone. It is strange that as yet I have not seen the Count eat or drink. He must be a very peculiar[4] man!

After breakfast, I did a little exploring[5] in the castle. Doors, doors, doors everywhere, and all locked. There are no exits except the windows. I am a prisoner!

As soon as I realized this, I heard a door below shut. I went cautiously[6] to my room and saw the Count making the bed. This only confirmed[7] my suspicions[8]: there are no servants in the house. Now I am sure it must have been the Count himself who drove the coach.

Why did all the people at Bistritz have some terrible fear[9] for me? Bless that good woman who hung the crucifix round my neck! It is a comfort[10] to me.

1. **wrench open** 扭開
   wrench [wentʃ] (v.) 猛扭
2. **fling out** 扔出去；丟出去
   (fling-flung-flung)
3. **shatter** [ˈʃætər] (v.) 粉碎
4. **peculiar** [pɪˈkjuːljər] (a.)
   乖僻的；奇怪的
5. **do exploring** 探索；探險
6. **cautiously** [ˈkɔːʃəsli]
   (adv.) 小心地；謹慎地

7. **confirm** [kənˈfɜːrm]
   (v.) 確認
8. **suspicion** [səˈspɪʃən]
   (n.) 懷疑
9. **fear** [fɪr] (n.) 害怕；恐懼
10. **comfort** [ˈkʌmfərt] (n.)
    安慰；慰問

✔ *Check Up*

Choose all the things that Jonathan finds out.

a All the doors and windows are locked.

b There are no servants in the house.

c The Count must have been the coach driver.

Ans: b, c

35

12 May

Last evening the Count began by asking me about legal[1] matters for shipping[2].

"Suppose" he said, "I wish to ship goods[3], say, to Newcastle or Durham or Dover. Would it be easier to hire[4] a lawyer to claim[5] these goods when they arrive?"

I explained to the best of my ability. When he was satisfied, he suddenly stood up and said, "Except for your first letter to Mr. Hawkins, have you written any letters?"

I answered that I had not.

1. **legal** [ˈliːgəl] (a.) 法律的
2. **shipping** [ˈʃɪpɪŋ] (n.) 裝運
3. **goods** [gʊdz] (n.) 貨物
4. **hire** [haɪr] (v.) 雇用
5. **claim** [kleɪm] (v.) 領取
6. **grow** [groʊ] (v.) 漸漸變成
7. **refusal** [rɪˈfjuːzəl] (n.) 拒絕
8. **serve** [sɜːrv] (v.) 服務
9. **bearing** [ˈberɪŋ] (n.) 舉止
10. **dread** [dred] (n.) 懼怕；擔心

"Then write now, my young friend," he said. "Write to Mr. Hawkins and any others that you shall stay with me until a month from now."

"Do you wish me to stay so long?" I asked, for my heart grew[6] cold at the thought.

"I will take no refusal[7]. Your employer sent you here to serve[8] me, did he not?"

What could I do but accept? It was Mr. Hawkins' interest, not mine, and I had to think of him, not myself.

Besides, while Count Dracula was speaking, there was something in his eyes and in his bearing[9] which made me remember that I was a prisoner and that even if I wished to leave, I could have no choice. So I wrote the letters with a growing sense of dread[10].

✓ Check Up

The Count wants Jonathan to _____.

  a write several letters
  b receive some goods in England
  c leave in two or three weeks

Ans: a

When he left me, I went to my room. After a little while, I looked out the window. I found some sense of freedom and peace in the vast[1] and beautiful view of the countryside, bathed[2] in yellow moonlight.

As I leaned from the window, my eye caught some movement below me. The Count's head was coming out from a lower window. At first, I was amused[3] by this coincidence[4], but my feelings changed to repulsion[5] and terror when I saw the whole man slowly emerge[6] from the window and begin to crawl[7] down the castle wall like some huge, black insect, face down with his cloak[8] spreading[9] out around him like great wings.

At first, I could not believe my eyes. I thought it was some trick[10] of the moonlight, but I kept looking, and it was no delusion[11].

---

1. **vast** [væst] (a.) 廣闊的
2. **bathe** [beɪð] (v.) 沐浴
3. **amuse** [əˈmjuːz] (v.) 使歡樂；使發笑
4. **coincidence** [koʊˈɪnsɪdəns] (n.) 巧合
5. **repulsion** [rɪˈpʌlʃən] (n.) 嫌惡；排斥
6. **emerge** [ɪˈmɜːrdʒ] (v.) 出現
7. **crawl** [krɔːl] (v.) 爬
8. **cloak** [kloʊk] (n.) 斗篷
9. **spread** [spred] (v.) 張開

What kind of man is this, or what kind of creature[12]? I feel the dread of this horrible place overpowering[13] me. I am in fear, in awful fear, and there is no escape[14] for me.

✅ Check Up

What does the Count remind Jonathan of?

ⓐ a lizard ⓑ an insect ⓒ a large bat

Ans: b

10. **trick** [trɪk] (n.) 惡作劇
11. **delusion** [dɪ'luːʒən] (n.) 迷惑；欺騙
12. **creature** ['kriːtʃər] (n.) 生物；動物

13. **overpower** [ˌoʊvər'paʊr] (v.) 使無法忍受；擊敗
14. **escape** [ɪ'skeɪp] (n.) 逃離

15 May

Once more I have seen the count go out in his insect-like fashion. When he did this, I decided to explore more of the castle. All the doors I tried were locked. At last, however, I found one door at the top of a stairway[1] that was unlocked but difficult to open. I exerted[2] all my strength[3] to push it open enough to permit[4] me to pass.

I found myself in a room that was probably used by the ladies of the castle long, long ago. I liked this room and its view, so I sat down to write in my diary.

Later: The morning of 16 May

I swear[5] I am not mad, but there are things here that put my sanity[6] to the test. It is maddening[7] to think that there are foul[8] beasts[9] here worse than the Count and that I must trust him to keep me safe as long as I am useful to him.

When the Count warned me against[10] falling asleep in other rooms besides my bedroom, I was frightened. But after I had written in my diary, I felt sleepy. I was still in the room at the top of the stairs. The moonlight was soft, and the couch in the room was inviting. I stretched[11] out on the couch and fell asleep.

1. **stairway** ['sterweɪ] (n.)
   樓梯;階梯
2. **exert** [ɪg'zɜːrt] (v.) 用（力）
3. **strength** [streŋθ] (n.) 力氣
4. **permit** [pər'mɪt] (v.) 允許
5. **swear** [swer] (v.) 發誓
6. **sanity** ['sænɪti] (n.)
   精神正常
7. **maddening** ['mædənɪŋ] (a.)
   令人發狂的
8. **foul** [faʊl] (a.) 邪惡的
9. **beast** [biːst] (n.) 野獸
10. **warn against** 提醒;警告
11. **stretch** [stretʃ] (v.) 伸懶腰

✅ Check Up
What realization does Jonathan come to?

- a There are rooms in the castle where he can sleep.
- b He needs the Count to protect him from other monsters.
- c There is a way to escape.

Ans: b

Suddenly, I woke, or I thought I did. Perhaps it was a dream, for there in the room with me were three ladies. It seemed like a dream because the ladies cast no shadow in the moonlight.

Two were dark and had great, dark, piercing[1] eyes that seemed to be almost red. The other was fair[2], with great masses of golden hair and eyes like pale[3] sapphires. All three had brilliant[4] white teeth that shone like pearls against the ruby of their full lips.

I felt longing[5] and at the same time deadly[6] fear. They whispered[7] together, and then all three of them laughed, such a silvery, musical laugh, but also inhumanly[8] hard. The fair girl shook her head coyly[9], and the other two urged her on.

One said, "Go on! You are first, and we shall follow. You have the right to begin."

The other added, "He is young and strong. There are kisses for us all."

---

1. **piercing** [ˈpɪrəsɪŋ] (a.) 銳利的
2. **fair** [fer] (a.) 白膚金髮的
3. **pale** [peɪl] (a.) 蒼白的
4. **brilliant** [ˈbrɪljənt] (a.) 明亮的
5. **longing** [ˈlɔːŋɪŋ] (a.) 渴望的
6. **deadly** [ˈdedli] (a.) 極度的
7. **whisper** [ˈwɪspər] (v.) 輕聲說
8. **inhumanly** [ɪnˈhjuːmənli] (adv.) 無人情味地
9. **coyly** [kɔɪli] (adv.) 羞怯地
10. **agony** [ˈægəni] (n.) 痛苦
11. **anticipation** [ænˌtɪsɪˈpeɪʃən] (n.) 預期
12. **advance** [ədˈvæns] (v.) 前進

I lay quiet, looking out from under my eyelashes in an agony[10] of delightful anticipation[11]. The fair girl advanced[12] and bent over me till I could smell her breath. It was bittersweet[13], smelling of honey but also faintly[14] of blood.

She was both thrilling[15] and repulsive[16], and as she arched[17] her neck, she actually licked her lips like an animal. Lower and lower went her head as her lips went below my chin and seemed to fasten on my throat. I could feel her hot breath on my neck. I closed my eyes and waited with a hammering[18] heart.

---

13. **bittersweet** [ˈbɪtərˌswiːt] (a.) 苦樂參半的

14. **faintly** [ˈfeɪntli] (adv.) 微弱地；模糊地

15. **thrilling** [ˈθrɪlɪŋ] (a.) 令人興奮的

16. **repulsive** [rɪˈpʌlsɪv] (a.) 令人厭惡的

17. **arch** [ɑːrtʃ] (v.) 拱起

18. **hammering** [ˈhæmərɪŋ] (a.) 錘擊的聲音

🎧15　　Ah, too suddenly, I was conscious of[1] the presence[2] of the Count, as if he were a storm in the room. I saw his strong hand grasp[3] the slender[4] neck of the fair woman and with a giant's power draw it back, her blue eyes transformed[5] with rage[6].

---

1. **be conscious of** 意識到
2. **presence** [ˈprezəns] (n.) 出現
3. **grasp** [græsp] (v.) 抓
4. **slender** [ˈslendər] (a.) 纖細的
5. **transform** [trænsˈfɔːrm] (v.) 改變；變換
6. **rage** [reɪdʒ] (n.) 狂怒；盛怒

But the Count! Never did I imagine such fury. His eyes were blazing red, like the flames[7] of hell[8]. He hurled[9] the woman from him, and then he raised his hand against the others.

In a voice that cut the air, he said, "How dare you touch him when I had forbidden[10] it? This man belongs to me!"

The Count then said in a soft whisper, "I promise you that when I am done with my young friend here, you may kiss him at your will. Now go!"

As I looked through half-shut[11] eyes, they seemed to fade[12] into the rays[13] of the moonlight and pass out through the window. Then the horror overcame me, and I sank down unconscious[14].

✓ *Check Up*

The Count promises the ladies they could kiss Jonathan
_____.

a when the Count is done with him
b after the Count kisses him
c before the Count comes in

Ans: a

7. **flame** [fleɪm] (n.) 火燄
8. **hell** [hel] (n.) 地獄
9. **hurl** [ˈhɜːrl] (v.) 猛力丟擲
10. **forbid** [fərˈbɪd] (v.) 禁止
11. **half-shut** [ˈhæfʃʌt] (a.) 半閉的
12. **fade** [feɪd] (v.) 離去；褪去
13. **ray** [reɪ] (n.) 光線
14. **unconscious** [ʌnˈkɑːnʃəs] (a.) 無意識的

19 May

The date of my death is approaching. Last night, the Count asked me in the nicest way to write three letters, one saying that my work here was nearly done, and that I should start for home within a few days; another that I was starting on the next morning from the time of the letter; and the third that I had left the castle and arrived at Bistritz.

I could not refuse, as I am totally[1] within the power of the Count.

I therefore[2] pretended[3] not to be worried, and I asked him what dates I should put on the letters. He said, "The first should be June 12, the second June 19, and the third June 29."

I know now the span[4] of my life. God help me!

1. **totally** [ˈtoʊtli] (adv.) 完全地
2. **therefore** [ˈðɛrfɔːr] (adv.) 因此
3. **pretend** [prɪˈtend] (v.) 假裝
4. **span** [spæn] (n.) 全長
5. **escape** [ɪˈskeɪp] (v.) 逃離
6. **band** [bænd] (n.) （一）夥
7. **attempt** [əˈtempt] (n.) 試圖
8. **communicate** [kəˈmjuːnɪkeɪt] (v.) 溝通
9. **polite** [pəˈlaɪt] (a.) 禮貌的
10. **ignore** [ɪɡˈnɔːr] (v.) 忽視

28 May

There is a chance to escape[5], or at least to send word home.
A band[6] of Gypsies have come to the castle. Perhaps they will help!

All attempts[7] to communicate[8] with the Gypsies have failed.
At first, they seemed very polite[9] to me as I shouted at them from my window. After a little while, however, they just ignored[10] me.

🎧 **17**

17 June

This morning, as I was sitting on the edge of my bed, I heard the cracking[1] of whips and the pounding[2] of horses' feet up the rocky[3] path.

With joy, I hurried to the window, and I saw two great wagons[4], each drawn by eight sturdy[5] horses, each driven by a Slovak[6], with wide hats, great nail-studded[7] belts, dirty sheep skins, and high boots.

I cried to them. They looked up at me stupidly, but the leader of the Gypsies said something, at which they laughed.

---

1. **cracking** [krækɪŋ] (n.) 霹啪作響
2. **pounding** [paʊndɪŋ] (n.) 腳步沉重
3. **rocky** [ˈrɑːki] (a.) 岩石的
4. **wagon** [ˈwægən] (n.) 馬車
5. **sturdy** [ˈstɜːrdi] (a.) 健壯的
6. **Slovak** [ˈsloʊvɑk] (n.) 斯洛伐克人

Afterward, no effort[8] of mine would make them even look at me. Their wagons contained[9] great, square boxes, with handles[10] of thick rope. These were evidently[11] empty by the way the Slovaks handled them. When they were all unloaded[12], the Slovaks rode off[13].

25 June

I must take action[14] of some sort during the day. I have not yet seen the Count in the daylight. Can it be that he sleeps when others are awake?

If I could only get into his room! There is a way, if one dares to take it. I have seen him crawl from his window. Why should not I imitate[15] him and go in by his window? It is a terrible risk[16], but I must take it.

✓ Check Up

What does Jonathan decide to do?

- a Hide in one of the big boxes.
- b Send a letter home with one of the Gypsies.
- c Climb out the window to find a way to escape.

Ans: c

---

7. **nail-studded** ['neɪl'stʌdɪd] (a.) 用釘子裝飾的
8. **effort** ['efərt] (n.) 努力
9. **contain** [kən'teɪn] (v.) 容納
10. **handle** ['hændl] (n.) 把手
11. **evidently** ['evɪdəntli] (adv.) 明顯地
12. **unload** [ʌn'loʊd] (v.) 卸貨
13. **ride off** 離開
14. **take action** 採取行動
15. **imitate** ['ɪmɪteɪt] (v.) 模仿
16. **risk** [rɪsk] (n.) 冒險；風險

Same day, later

I was successful. When I entered the Count's room, it was completely[1] empty except for a great pile[2] of gold in one corner, coins from all countries and ages. The large, heavy door was open, and I searched around the old, rundown[3] castle. Finally, in the basement[4], I made a discovery.

In one of the underground rooms, I saw about fifty great boxes half filled with newly dug[5] earth. Most were uncovered[6], and in one lay the Count!

My blood ran cold, but it seemed as if he were dead or asleep. His lips were as red as ever. But there was no sign[7] of movement, no pulse[8], no breath, and no beating[9] of the heart.

1. **completely** [kəmˈpliːtli] (adv.) 完全地；徹底地
2. **pile** [paɪl] (n.) 堆
3. **rundown** [ˈrʌndaʊn] (a.) 破敗的；失修的
4. **basement** [ˈbeɪsmənt] (n.) 地下室
5. **dig** [dɪg] (n.) 挖 (dig-dug-dug)
6. **uncovered** [ʌnˈkʌvərd] (a.) 未加蓋的
7. **sign** [saɪn] (n.) 跡象；顯示
8. **pulse** [pʌls] (n.) 脈搏
9. **beating** [ˈbiːtɪŋ] (n.) 心跳
10. **search** [sɜːrtʃ] (v.) 尋找
11. **flee** [fliː] (v.) 逃走 (flee-fled-fled)
12. **regain** [rɪˈgeɪn] (v.) 返回
13. **pant** [pænt] (v.) 喘氣

I thought he might have the keys on him, but when I went to search[10], I saw his dead eyes and in them such a look of hate that I fled[11] from the place.

Leaving the Count's room by the window, I crawled again up the castle wall. Regaining[12] my room, I threw myself panting[13] upon the bed and tried to think.

✓ *Check Up* True or False.

a The Count had died and was no longer a problem. _____
b Jonathan found a lot of gold. _____
c Jonathan became scared and ran back to his room. _____

19 *29 June*

Today I fell asleep in the library and was awakened by the Count, who looked at me grimly[1].

He said, "Tomorrow, my friend, we must part[2]. You return to your beautiful England, and I to my work. When my workers and I have gone, my carriage shall come for you and shall bear[3] you to the Borgo Pass to meet the coach from Bukovina to Bistritz."

---

1. **grimly** [grɪmli] (adv.) 可怕地
2. **part** [pɑːrt] (v.) 分開；離別
3. **bear** [ber] (v.) 運送；攜帶
   (bear-bore-born)

4. **diabolical** [ˌdaɪəˈbɑːlɪkəl] (a.) 惡魔的；殘忍的
5. **trick** [trɪk] (n.) 把戲；惡作劇

I didn't believe him, and I asked, "Why may I not go tonight?"

He smiled, such a soft, smooth, diabolical[4] smile that I knew there was some trick[5] behind his smoothness[6]. He moved to the window and said, "Wait! Listen carefully!"

Outside came the howling[7] of many wolves. It was almost as if the sound sprang up[8] as soon as he raised his hand. I knew there was no escape[9] at night when such creatures as these roamed[10] the woods[11].

After a minute or two, I went to my own room. The last I saw of Count Dracula was his kissing his hand to me, with a red light of triumph[12] in his eyes.

☑️ Check Up

Why couldn't Jonathan leave that night?

- a There were mountain lions in the dark.
- b The coach driver was not available.
- c There were too many wolves in the forest.

6. **smoothness** ['smuːðnɪs] (n.) 和善
7. **howling** ['haʊlɪŋ] (n.) 嚎叫
8. **spring up** 出現 (spring-sprang-sprung)
9. **escape** [ɪ'skeɪp] (n.) 逃離
10. **roam** [roʊm] (v.) 遊蕩
11. **woods** [wʊdz] (n.) 樹林
12. **triumph** ['traɪəmf] (n.) 勝利

30 June

These may be the last words I ever write in this diary. Today, I climbed down the wall again. I made my way[1] to the box with the Count in it. This time, it was covered, but the nails were not hammered in yet. I needed the key to the front gate, so I moved the lid[2] aside, but then I had a shock[3].

There lay the Count, looking as if his youth[4] had been half restored[5]. His mouth was redder than ever, for on his lips was fresh blood, which trickled[6] from the corners of his mouth and ran down over his chin and neck. He seemed like a fat leech[7], resting after gorging[8] himself on blood.

1. **make one's way** 前進；行進
2. **lid** [lɪd] (n.) 蓋子
3. **shock** [ʃɑːk] (n.) 震驚
4. **youth** [juːθ] (n.) 朝氣
5. **restore** [rɪˈstɔːr] (v.) 修復；復原
6. **trickle** [ˈtrɪkəl] (v.) 滴
7. **leech** [liːtʃ] (n.) 水蛭
8. **gorge** [gɔːrdʒ] (v.) 塞飽
9. **shudder** [ˈʃʌdər] (v.) 發抖；顫慄
10. **bend over** 彎下身 (bend-bent-bent)
11. **revolt** [rɪˈvoʊlt] (v.) 厭惡；反感
12. **contact** [ˈkɑːntækt] (n.) 碰觸
13. **merry** [ˈmeri] (a.) 愉快的；欣喜的
14. **dreadful** [ˈdredfəl] (a.) 可怕的；令人恐懼的
15. **entry** [ˈentri] (n.) 留筆

I shuddered[9] as I bent over[10] to touch him, and every sense in me revolted[11] at the contact[12], but I had to search. I felt everywhere, but there was no key. While I stood there thinking, I heard the Gypsies' merry[13] voices coming down the tunnel.

Quickly, I ran and climbed back up to my room. Soon, I heard the sound of the Gypsy wagons leaving. I am alone in the castle with those horrible women. I shall try to climb down the castle wall to the courtyard. I must find a way from this dreadful[14] place.

If this is indeed my last entry[15], goodbye all! I love you, Mina!

A Circle the words best describe the character of "Dracula".

1 very pale skin

2 not very good with English

3 wide, kind smile

4 thick eyebrows

5 long, narrow fingers

6 long, white teeth

B Fill in the blanks with the given words.

Three women	Gypsies	Slovaks

1 _____ delivered empty boxes to the castle.

2 _____ prepared the boxes for transportation.

3 _____ tried to drink Jonathan's blood.

C True or False.

T F 1 The Count has many servants in his castle.

T F 2 Jonathan never sees the Count eat or drink.

T F 3 The Count wants to buy a large, old mansion in London.

T F 4 The innkeeper and his wife don't speak any German.

T F 5 Jonathan bought a crucifix in Bistritz.

D Choose the correct answer.

❶ Why did Jonathan Harker travel to Translyvania?

(a) He was interested in buying some property there.

(b) He was sent by his office to help a client.

(c) He went there to learn a foreign language.

❷ Why did Jonathan think Dracula and his driver were actually the same person?

(a) They both had long beards.

(b) They were both very strong.

(c) They both had hands with unnatural strength.

❸ How will Jonathan try to escape from the castle?

(a) He will climb down the wall.

(b) He will try to break the door down.

(c) He will hide in one of the boxes.

E Rearrange the sentences in chronological order.

❶ Jonathan sees the Count crawl down the wall of the castle.

❷ The Count breaks Jonathan's mirror.

❸ Jonathan writes three letters to England.

❹ Jonathan finds some boxes under the castle.

❺ Three women find Jonathan asleep.

_____ ⇨ _____ ⇨ _____ ⇨ _____ ⇨ _____

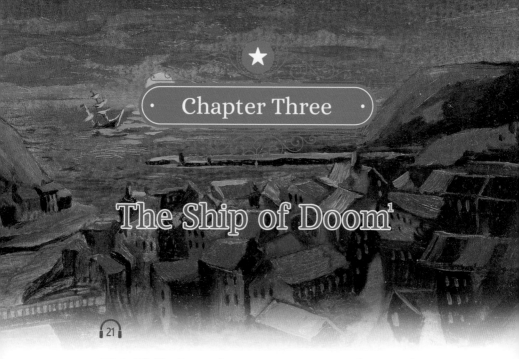

· Chapter Three ·

The Ship of Doom[1]

🎧 21

While Jonathan was in Transylvania, his fiancee[2] Mina and her best friend, Lucy, were exchanging letters about Lucy's recent engagement[3] to an English gentleman named Arthur Holmwood.

Mina was happy for Lucy, but she was also getting a little worried about Jonathan. He had been gone for a very long time and had only sent short letters.

---

1. **doom** [duːm] (n.) 厄運
2. **fiancee** [ˌfiːɑːnˈseɪ] (n.) 未婚妻
3. **engagement** [ɪnˈgeɪdʒmənt] (n.) 訂婚
4. **relieve** [rɪˈliːv] (v.) 舒緩
5. **vacation** [veɪˈkeɪʃən] (v.) 度假
6. **guesthouse** [ˈgestˌhaʊs] (n.) 旅館

To celebrate Lucy's engagement and to relieve[4] Mina's worries for Jonathan, the two young women decided to vacation[5] together at a small seaside town named Whitby. They rented a room in a guesthouse[6] that overlooked[7] the sea, a small church, and its adjacent[8] graveyard[9].

Mina and Lucy became used to sitting on the tombstones[10] in the graveyard because the view was fantastic. One day, as Mina was sitting alone, a sailor came by[11]. He stopped to talk, but he kept looking at a strange ship far out to sea.

"That ship is sailing very strangely," he said. "She's a Russian ship, by the look of her. But she's moving about[12] in the oddest way. She changes direction[13] with every puff[14] of wind as if no one is steering[15] her. We'll hear more about her before this time tomorrow."

7. **overlook** [ˌoʊvərˈlʊk]
   (v.) 俯瞰；眺望
8. **adjacent** [əˈdʒeɪsənt]
   (a.) 相鄰的
9. **graveyard** [ˈɡreɪvjɑːrd]
   (n.) 墓園
10. **tombstone**
    [ˈtuːmstoʊn] (n.) 墓碑

11. **come by** 從旁經過
12. **move about** 四處走動
13. **direction** [dɪˈrekʃən]
    (n.) 方向
14. **puff** [pʌf] (n.) 一陣陣地吹
15. **steer** [stɪr] (v.) 駕駛

The sailor's prediction[1] was right, for the next day after a terrible storm, Mina read the following article in the Whitby town newspaper:

August 8

One of the greatest and most sudden storms on record has just been experienced[2] here, with results both strange and unique.

Shortly before ten o'clock, the stillness[3] of the hot and humid[4] air grew quite oppressive[5]. A little after midnight, a strange sound came from over the sea. Without warning, the storm broke so quickly it seemed most unnatural.

The waves rose in growing fury, transforming the flat[6], calm waters into a roaring[7] and devouring[8] monster. The wind roared like thunder and blew with such force that even strong men had difficulty standing up.

1. **prediction** [prɪˈdɪkʃən] (n.) 預測
2. **experience** [ɪkˈspɪriəns] (v.) 經歷
3. **stillness** [ˈstɪlnɪs] (n.) 靜止不動
4. **humid** [ˈhjuːmid] (a.) 潮濕的
5. **oppressive** [əˈpresɪv] (a.) 悶的
6. **flat** [flæt] (a.) 平的；平坦的
7. **roaring** [rɔːrɪŋ] (a.) 吼叫的
8. **devouring** [dɪˈvaʊrɪŋ] (a.) 吞沒的
9. **clammy** [ˈklæmi] (a.) 濕冷的
10. **onlooker** [ˈɑːnˌlʊkər] (n.) 觀眾；旁觀者
11. **drowned** [draʊnd] (a.) 溺斃的

A sea mist came in, cold and clammy[9], that made many onlookers[10] imagine that these were the ghosts of drowned[11] sailors. At times this mist cleared, and lightning flashes revealed waves as high as small mountains.

Small fishing boats were glimpsed[12] as they made a mad dash[13] into port. The new searchlight on the East Cliff, which was recently installed[14], was made to work. As each boat arrived safely, the crowd of onlookers let out[15] a great cheer[16].

Then the searchlight[17] caught a sight that made everyone gasp in fear. The foreign cargo[18] ship spotted[19] earlier before the storm was now much closer and in terrible danger of running aground[20] on the reef[21].

12. **glimpse** [glɪmps] (v.) 瞥見
13. **make a dash** 撞擊
14. **install** [ɪn'stɔːl] (v.) 安裝；設置
15. **let out** 洩露
16. **cheer** [tʃɪr] (n.) 歡呼；喝采
17. **searchlight** ['sɜːrtʃlaɪt] (n.) 探照燈
18. **cargo** ['kɑːrgoʊ] (n.) 貨物
19. **spot** [spɑːt] (v.) 發現

20. **aground** [ə'graʊnd] (adv.) 擱淺；觸礁
21. **reef** [riːf] (n.) 礁岩

61

23 Then came another mass of sea fog, greater than anyone could remember, which cut off all sight of the impending[1] disaster[2]. The rays of the searchlight were kept fixed[3] in the direction of the reef, where the sound of the shock was expected.

The wind suddenly shifted[4] to the northeast, and the sea fog was blasted[5] away. Between the piers[6], leaping from wave to wave as it rushed[7] at headlong[8] speed, swept[9] the strange schooner[10] before this new wind with all her sails set. It gained the safety of the harbor as the searchlight followed her. This light revealed a sight that made every onlooker shudder in horror. Lashed[11] to the wheel of the ship was a corpse[12], with a drooping[13] head that swung[14] horribly to and fro at each motion of the ship. No other

1. **impending** [ɪmˈpɛndɪŋ] (a.) 即將發生的
2. **disaster** [dɪˈzæstər] (n.) 災難
3. **fixed** [fɪkst] (a.) 固定的
4. **shift** [ʃɪft] (v.) 轉移
5. **blast away** 吹走
6. **pier** [pɪr] (n.) 凸式碼頭
7. **rush** [rʌʃ] (v.) 奔騰；突然出現
8. **headlong** [ˈhedlɔːŋ] (a.) 猛然的
9. **sweep** [swiːp] (v.) 襲捲
10. **schooner** [ˈskuːnər] (n.) （雙桅以上的）縱帆船
11. **lash** [læʃ] (v.) 用繩捆綁
12. **corpse** [kɔːrps] (n.) 屍體
13. **drooping** [druːpɪŋ] (a.) 下垂的
14. **swing** [swɪŋ] (v.) 搖擺
15. **deck** [dek] (n.) 甲板
16. **awe** [ɔː] (n.) 敬畏；畏怯
17. **chapel** [ˈtʃæpəl] (n.) 小禮拜堂

person, dead or alive, could be seen on the deck[15] at all.

A great awe[16] came over everyone as they realized this ship had found the safety of the harbor at the hands of a dead man. However, the ship could not slow down. It sped past the piers and hit the sandy beach just under the Whitby chapel[17] with a terrific[18] crash[19].

In the next day's paper, there appeared a follow-up article:

The coastguard[20] has identified[21] the mystery ship that ran aground during the storm as the Demeter, a Russian ship out of Varna. The corpse tied to the wheel was the captain, and his logbook[22] was found nearby.

18. **terrific** [təˈrɪfɪk] (a.)
可怕的；嚇人的

19. **crash** [kræʃ] (n.) 撞擊

20. **coastguard** [ˈkoʊstgɑːrd]
(n.) 海岸巡邏員

21. **identify** [aɪˈdentəfaɪ] (v.)
確定；辨識

22. **logbook** [ˈlɔːɡˌbʊk] (n.)
航海日記

63

Legends of Vampires[1]

Bram Stoker created the world's most famous vampire, but he was not the first person to think about vampires. Legends[2] about vampires have appeared in many cultures for thousands of years. In Indian folklore[3], there is a creature called Rakshasa that acts like a vampire. Rakshasas appear as humans with some animal features like claws[4] or fangs[5]. They not only drink their victim's[6] blood, but also eat the flesh[7]! They could only be killed by fire, sunlight or a religious ceremony that would kill its spirit.

1. **vampire** ['væmpaɪr] (n.) 吸血鬼
2. **legend** ['lɛdʒənd] (n.) 傳說
3. **folklore** ['foʊklɔːr] (n.)
   民間傳說
4. **claw** [klɔː] (n.) 爪子
5. **fang** [fæŋ] (n.) 毒牙
6. **victim** ['vɪktɪm] (n.) 受害者
7. **flesh** [flɛʃ] (n.) 肉
8. **curse** [kɜːrs] (n.) 詛咒
9. **puberty** ['pjuːbərti] (n.) 青春期
10. **garlic** ['gɑːrlɪk] (n.) 大蒜
11. **mysteriously** [mɪ'stɪriəsli]
    (adv.) 神秘地；不可思議地
12. **influence** ['ɪnfluːəns] (v.) 影響

In Mexico, vampires were mostly female. They were called Tlahuelpuchi. They were born with the curse[8] of being a vampire, but they did not know it until they reached puberty[9]. These vampires had to drink the blood of a baby once a month, or they would die. Garlic[10], onions and metal were used to make these vampires go away.

During the Dark Ages in Europe, when a person died suddenly and mysteriously[11] in his or her sleep, people began to say that vampires must have killed that person. In this way, vampires represented Death. In order to stop the deaths, villagers would dig up graves to look for the "vampire." Bodies that were not decayed were thought to be the vampire responsible for the deaths in the village. To "kill" the vampire, villagers then cut off the body's head, or removed the heart. These European legends influenced[12] Bram Stoker in his creation of Count Dracula.

Chapter Four

🎧 24 Danger in the Night

MINA MURRAY'S JOURNAL

10 August

The funeral[1] of the poor sea captain today was most touching[2]. Everyone here thinks the captain was a hero, even if it did seem that he became mad in the end. But he brought his ship in to port[3] even after he died.

Poor Lucy seems very upset. She is restless[4] all the time. I think she is having terrible dreams, but she will not speak of them. When she was young, Lucy would sleepwalk[5]. Now she is starting again.

---

1. **funeral** ['fjuːnərəl] (n.) 喪禮
2. **touching** ['tʌtʃɪŋ] (a.) 感人的
3. **port** [pɔːrt] (n.) 港口
4. **restless** ['restləs] (a.) 得不到休息的
5. **sleepwalk** ['slipwɔːk] (v.) 夢遊
6. **figure** ['fɪgjər] (n.) 人影
7. **fasten** ['fæsən] (v.) 繫；綁
8. **prick** [prɪk] (v.) 刺傷

12 August

Last night, I woke and found Lucy gone from our bedroom! I walked to the church where we liked to sit. I saw a figure[6] dressed in white lying on a tombstone. As I got nearer, I saw a dark figure bent over her. I yelled and ran forward, and the figure turned to me. I could see red, hateful eyes and a pale face.

Then the figure vanished, and I found Lucy asleep on the tombstone. I fastened[7] a cloak around her shoulders. In doing so, I must have pricked[8] her with the pin, for there were drops of blood on her neck.

✓ *Check Up* What did Lucy do when she was young?

a She used to walk in her sleep.

b She used to sleep on the floor of her room.

c She used to make up stories about monsters.

25

14 August

Lucy has gotten worse. She wakes up in the middle of[1] the night and tries to leave the room. She is very pale[2] and weak during the day.

I have finally received a letter from Jonathan. He is ill in a hospital in Budapest. I must go to him, but I am afraid of leaving Lucy alone. So I have sent word to her fiance, Arthur. He is coming soon and has promised to take Lucy and her mother to his London estate. As soon as he arrives, I must leave for Budapest. I do hope Lucy recovers[3] while I am gone!

24 August

After a long trip, I arrived at Jonathan's hospital in Budapest. He is weak and tired, but alive. He has had some terrible shock. When he woke, he asked me for his coat, as he wanted to get something from the pocket. I saw his journal. He saw me looking at it, and after a moment, he held my hand and told me he loved me dearly.

1. **in the middle of**
   在……當中
2. **pale** [peɪl] (a.) 蒼白的
3. **recover** [rɪˈkʌvər] (v.)
   恢復；康復
4. **ordeal** [ɔːrˈdiːl] (n.)
   苦難；折磨
5. **survive** [sərˈvaɪv] (v.) 存活

Then he said I should read his journal, but he never wanted to discuss it ever again. So I learned about Jonathan's ordeal[4] at Castle Dracula. It is so strange, but I will not discuss it with him. He survived[5], and we are together.

✓ *Check Up*

What did Mina do when she received Jonathan's letter?

   [a] She ignored the letter and stayed with Lucy.

   [b] She left for Budapest.

   [c] She took Lucy to see Jonathan.

Ans: b

26

2 September

Jonathan has recovered much of his previous health and vigor[1]. We were married yesterday in a small Budapest church! We are so much in love. Tomorrow we begin the long journey back to England.

And so Mina and Jonathan returned to London to start their new life together. However, when they arrived, Mina found a letter from Arthur Holmwood waiting for her. The letter contained tragic[2] news: Lucy had died!

1. **vigor** [ˈvɪɡər] (n.) 活力
2. **tragic** [ˈtrædʒɪk] (a.) 不幸的；悲劇的
3. **merry** [ˈmeri] (a.) 愉快的
4. **tiredness** [ˈtaɪrdnɪs] (n.) 疲倦
5. **plague** [pleɪɡ] (v.) 折磨
6. **fall ill** 生病 (fall-fell-fallen)

Arthur Holmwood's Story

Lucy and her mother came to live with me in London. At first, she seemed merry[3] and did not show any signs of the tiredness[4] or weakness that had plagued[5] her in Whitby. But after a week, she suddenly fell ill[6] and would not leave her bed.

I sent for my dear friend, the physician[7] Dr. Jack Seward, who came at once[8]. He found two small, strange wounds[9] on her neck and determined[10] that she had lost a lot of blood. But how? There was not a drop of blood in her bed!

At a loss[11] for an explanation, Dr. Seward called on[12] his old professor, Dr. Abraham Van Helsing. This learned[13] man was gracious[14] enough to come at once after he heard the details[15] of Lucy's case.

7. **physician** [fɪˈzɪʃən] (n.) 醫師；內科醫生
8. **at once** 立刻；馬上
9. **wound** [waʊnd] (n.) 傷口
10. **determine** [dɪˈtɜːrmɪn] (v.) 判定
11. **at a loss** 困惑不解

12. **call on** 請求
13. **learned** [ˈlɜːrnɪd] (a.) 博學的
14. **gracious** [ˈgreɪʃəs] (a.) 仁慈的；和藹的
15. **detail** [dɪˈteɪl] (n.) 詳情

🎧 27

When Dr. Van Helsing arrived, we all went to Lucy's room. She was ghastly[1] pale. The red seemed to have gone even from her lips and gums[2], and the bones of her face stood out prominently[3]. Her breathing was painful to hear. Lucy lay motionless[4] and did not seem to have strength to speak, so for a while we were all silent. Then Van Helsing beckoned[5], and we went gently out of the room.

The instant we had closed the door, he said, "My God! This is dreadful. There is no time to be lost. She will die for sheer[6] want of blood. There must be a transfusion[7] of blood at once. Arthur, you are the youngest and strongest of us three."

He did not have to speak further. I swore that Lucy could have my blood, down to the last drop if need be. Dr. Van Helsing performed[8] the transfusion immediately. Apparently[9], his technique was correct. With my blood coursing[10] in Lucy's veins[11], she showed a marked[12] improvement[13].

---

1. **ghastly** [ˈgæstli] (a.) 死人般的
2. **gum** [gʌm] (n.) 牙齦；牙床
3. **prominently** [ˈprɑːmɪnəntli] (adv.) 顯著地
4. **motionless** [ˈmouʃənləs] (a.) 不動的；靜止的
5. **beckon** [ˈbekən] (v.) 示意
6. **sheer** [ʃɪr] (a.) 全然的
7. **transfusion** [trænsˈfjuːʒən] (n.) 輸血
8. **perform** [pərˈfɔːrm] (v.) 執行；履行

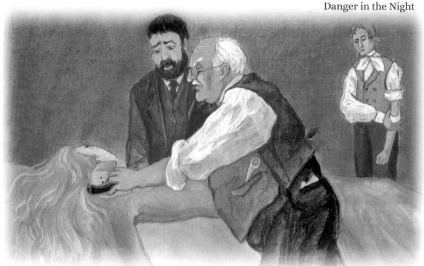

The next day, I had to leave for my father's house outside London. He was gravely[14] ill, and I needed to see him. Reluctantly[15], I left Lucy in the care of Dr. Seward and Dr. Van Helsing. They seem capable of bringing Lucy back to good health.

✔ *Check Up*

Why did Arthur leave Lucy?

- a He had to go on a business trip.
- b He had to take care of his sick father.
- c He needed to find a new doctor.

Ans: b

---

9. **apparently** [əˈpærəntli] (adv.) 顯然地

10. **course** [kɔːrs] (v.) 流動

11. **vein** [veɪn] (n.) 血管

12. **marked** [mɑːrkt] (a.) 明顯的

13. **improvement** [ɪmˈpruːvmənt] (n.) 改善

14. **gravely** [ˈɡreɪvli] (adv.) 嚴重地

15. **reluctantly** [rɪˈlʌktəntli] (adv.) 不情願地

Dr. Seward's Story

Shortly after Arthur left to attend[1] his ill father, Van Helsing told me he needed to return to his home in Amsterdam to fetch[2] some books related to[3] Lucy's illness.

"I will only be gone a few days," he told me. "Watch over[4] Lucy, especially at night. Put a chair near her bed and do not let her[5] sleepwalk! This is of extreme[6] importance. If you must sleep, sleep during the day."

He would not give me any explanation for this strange request, only saying that he needed to consult[7] the books he left in his apartment.

When I told Lucy's mother that Dr. Van Helsing had directed that I should sit up[8] with Lucy, she almost pooh-poohed[9] the idea, pointing out her daughter's renewed[10] strength and excellent spirits[11]. I was firm[12], however, and made preparations for my long vigil[13].

1. attend [əˈtɛnd] (v.) 照料
2. fetch [fɛtʃ] (v.) 去拿來
3. related to 與……有關
4. watch over 留心
5. let+ A + 讓……做（事）
6. extreme [ɪkˈstriːm] (a.) 極度的；非常的
7. consult [kənˈsʌlt] (v.) 查閱
8. sit up 熬夜
9. pooh-pooh [puːˈpuː] (v.) 表示輕視、不屑
10. renew [rɪˈnuː] (v.) 恢復
11. spirit [ˈspɪrɪt] (n.) 精神
12. firm [fɜːrm] (a.) 堅決的
13. vigil [ˈvɪdʒɪl] (n.) 守夜
14. object [ɑːbˈdʒɛkt] (v.) 反對
15. gratefully [ˈɡreɪtfəli] (adv.) 感激地

Lucy did not in any way object[14], but she looked at me gratefully[15] whenever I caught her eye. After a long while she seemed to sink[16] off to sleep, but with an effort[17] she seemed to pull herself together and shook it off. It was apparent[18] that she did not want to sleep, so I tackled[19] the subject at once.

"You do not want to sleep?"

"No. I am afraid."

"But, my dear girl, you may sleep tonight. I am here watching you, and I can promise that nothing will happen."

"How good you are to me. Then I will sleep!" And as soon as she said "sleep," she sighed[20] in relief[21] and sank back, asleep.

16. **sink** [sɪŋk] (v.) 陷入 (sink-sank-sunk)
17. **with an effort** 努力
18. **apparent** [əˈpærənt] (a.) 明顯的
19. **tackle** [ˈtækəl] (v.) 處理
20. **sigh** [saɪ] (v.) 嘆氣
21. **in relief** 放鬆；寬心

All night long I watched over her. She never stirred[1] but slept on and on in a deep, tranquil[2], life-giving[3] sleep. There was a smile on her face, and it was evident[4] that no bad dreams had come to disturb[5] her peace of mind.

For two nights, I watched over Lucy. During the day, I tended[6] my regular duties[7] at the mental[8] asylum where I work. This schedule began to take its toll[9] on me. On the third night, I arrived at Arthur's estate and found that Lucy was up and in cheerful spirits.

When she shook hands with me, she looked sharply at my face and said, "No sitting up tonight for you. You are worn out. I am quite well again. Indeed, I am, and if there is to be any sitting up, it is I who will sit up with you."

I would not argue the point but went and had my supper. Then Lucy took me upstairs and showed me a room next to her own, where a cozy[10] fire was burning.

"Now," she said, "You must stay here. I shall leave this door open and my door, too. You can lie on the sofa. If I want anything, I shall call out[11], and you can come to me at once."

I could not but[12] agree, for I was dog-tired[13] and could not have sat up had I tried. So, after making her renew[14] her promise to call me if she needed anything, I lay on the sofa and forgot all about everything.

1. **stir** [stɜːr] (v.) 移動
   (stir-stirred-stirred)
2. **tranquil** [ˈtræŋkwɪl] (a.)
   平穩的；穩定的
3. **life-giving** [ˈlaɪfˌɡɪvɪŋ] (a.)
   恢復生氣的
4. **evident** [ˈevɪdənt] (a.)
   明顯的；明白的
5. **disturb** [dɪˈstɜːrb] (v.)
   擾亂；妨礙
6. **tend** [tend] (v.) 照料；管理

7. **duty** [ˈduːti] (n.)
   職責；職務
8. **mental asylum** 精神病院
9. **take one's toll** 付出代價
10. **cozy** [ˈkoʊzi] (a.) 舒適的
11. **call out** 叫出來
12. **cannot but** 不得不
13. **dog-tired** [ˈdɔːɡˈtaɪrd] (a.)
    筋疲力盡的
14. **renew** [rɪˈnuː] (v.)
    重申；重複

30

I was conscious of[1] the professor's hand on my head, and started awake in a second.

"And how is our patient?" he said.

"Let us see," I replied.

When we entered Lucy's room, we saw a terrible sight. There on the bed lay poor Lucy, more horribly white than ever. Even her lips were white, and her gums seemed to have shrunk[2] back from her teeth, as we sometimes see in a corpse after a prolonged[3] illness.

Van Helsing immediately felt for her heartbeat[4].

"It is not too late," he said. "It beats, but feebly[5]. All our work is undone[6]. We must begin again. There is no young Arthur here now. I have to call on you yourself this time, friend John."

He performed another blood transfusion, using my blood this time. Lucy slept well into the day, and when she woke, she was fairly well and strong, though not nearly so much so as the day before.

---

1. **be conscious of** 意識到
2. **shrink** [ʃrɪŋk] (v.) 收縮；皺縮 (shrink-shrank-shrunk)
3. **prolonged** [prəˈlɔːŋd] (a.) 拖延的
4. **heartbeat** [ˈhɑːrtbiːt] (n.) 心跳
5. **feebly** [ˈfiːbli] (adv.) 衰弱地
6. **undone** [ʌnˈdʌn] (a.) 沒有做的；毀了的

That evening, Dr. Van Helsing gave Lucy a necklace of what looked like flowers. At first she was delighted[7], but then she said, "Oh, Professor, I believe you are playing a joke on[8] me. Why, these flowers are only common garlic."

"Not so, my dear!" replied Dr. Van Helsing sternly[9]. "I never jest[10]! There is a grim[11] purpose in what I do. Now sit still[12] a while. Come with me, friend John, and you shall help me deck[13] the room with garlic."

Check Up

How was Lucy when Van Helsing returned?

- a She was in good health.
- b She seemed very tired.
- c She was nearly dead.

Ans: c

---

7. **delighted** [dɪ'laɪtɪd] (a.) 欣喜的

8. **play a joke on** 開玩笑

9. **sternly** ['stɜːrnli] (adv.) 嚴厲地

10. **jest** [dʒest] (v.) 開玩笑

11. **grim** [grɪm] (a.) 堅決的

12. **still** [stɪl] (a.) 不動的；靜止的

13. **deck** [dek] (v.) 裝飾

31

The professor's actions were certainly odd and not to be found in any book that I had ever heard of. First, he fastened the windows and latched[1] them securely[2]. Next, taking a handful[3] of the flowers, he rubbed[4] them all over the sashes. Then he rubbed garlic all over the doorknob[5], above, below, and at each side, and around the fireplace in the same way.

When Lucy was ready in bed, he fixed a wreath[6] of garlic around her neck. The last words he said to her were, "Take care you do not disturb[7] it, and even if the air feels stuffy[8], do not open the window or the door."

1. **latch** [lætʃ] (v.) 閂上
2. **securely** [sɪˈkjʊrli] (adv.) 安全地;牢固地
3. **handful** [ˈhændfʊl] (n.) 一把
4. **rub** [rʌb] (v.) 擦拭
5. **doorknob** [ˈdɔːrnɑːb] (n.) 門把
6. **wreath** [riːθ] (n.) 花圈;花環

"I promise," said Lucy. "And thank you both a thousand times! Oh, what have I done to be blessed with such friends?"

As we left the house, Van Helsing said, "Tonight I can sleep in peace after two nights of travel and much reading in the day between. Tomorrow in the morning call for me, and we will see our pretty miss."

The next morning, we arrived early and met Lucy's mother. She told us that she had entered Lucy's room and found the air thick with the smell of garlic. Worried, she opened the window and took the necklace of garlic away from Lucy's neck.

As she spoke, Van Helsing's face turned ashen[9] gray. He did not speak a word to the mother, but as soon as she left, he sat down heavily in a chair.

✓ Check Up

Check all the things Van Helsing did to Lucy's room.

- a He put a guard outside the door.
- b He put a necklace of garlic around Lucy's neck.
- c He rubbed garlic flowers all around each entrance to the room.

Ans: b, c

7. **disturb** [dɪ'stɜːrb] (v.) 擾亂
8. **stuffy** ['stʌfi] (a.) 悶熱的
9. **ashen** ['æʃən] (a.) 面色蒼白的

32

"God! God! God!" he said. "What has this poor mother done? In her ignorance[1], in her desire[2] to give her daughter fresh air, she has lost her daughter's body and soul!"

But just as suddenly, his fit[3] of despair[4] left, and he jumped to his feet.

"Quick. We must act!" he said. "It is I now who must donate[5] the blood for Lucy's transfusion."

Again, we performed the transfusion, and again we saw health flow back into Lucy's pale and waxen[6] cheeks.

After the transfusion, we left Lucy sleeping peacefully in her bed. I had to return to the asylum to catch up on[7] my work, in which I was falling behind. That afternoon, I did not receive a summons[8] from Van Helsing, so with a weary[9] body, I headed home for a good night's rest.

In the morning, I had a shock. A telegram[10] arrived, dated the previous day from Van Helsing.

1. **ignorance** [ˈɪɡnərəns] (n.) 忽略；忽視
2. **desire** [dɪˈzaɪr] (n.) 渴望
3. **fit** [fɪt] (n.) （感情的）突發
4. **despair** [dɪˈsper] (n.) 絕望
5. **donate** [ˈdoʊneɪt] (v.) 捐贈

It read:

> *I must travel on errand*[11]. *Do not fail to watch over Lucy tonight. Very important.*

My God! I was supposed to[12] be with her last night! In a panic, I left for Arthur's estate at once. On arriving, I ran into Van Helsing, who was just arriving himself.

"What?" he said. "Did you not spend the night here? Didn't you get my telegram?"

We tried ringing the front bell, but there was no answer. Frightened, we ran to the rear[13] of the house and looked in the kitchen windows. The four servants were lying on the floor as if dead. Van Helsing broke the window, and we rushed in. From their labored[14] breathing and the smell of an open bottle of wine, we quickly realized they had been drugged.

---

6. **waxen** [ˈwæksən] (a.) 蒼白的
7. **catch up on** 趕完
8. **summons** [ˈsʌmənz] (n.) 召喚
9. **weary** [ˈwɪri] (a.) 疲憊的
10. **telegram** [ˈtelɪɡræm] (n.) 電報

11. **on errand** 辦事
12. **be supposed to** 應該
13. **rear** [rɪr] (n.) 後面
14. **labored** [ˈleɪbərd] (a.) 吃力的

33

We ran to Lucy's room and threw open the doors. How shall I describe[1] what we saw? On the bed lay Lucy and her mother. The mother's white face had a look of terror upon it. She must have died from[2] a heart attack[3]. By her side lay Lucy, her skin as white as chalk and her throat bare[4], showing the two little wounds[5] looking horribly white and mangled[6].

Without a word, the professor bent over Lucy, listening for life. Then, leaping to his feet, he cried out to me, "It is not yet too late! Quick! Wake the servants!"

Van Helsing had them prepare a hot bath for Lucy and told me to send for Arthur.

That afternoon, Arthur returned in a grim mood. His father had just passed away[7], and now his fiancee was on the edge of death. He went to her room and knelt[8] by her bed. She was barely[9] awake, and when she saw Arthur, she said, "My dear, bend closer so that I may kiss you."

---

1. **describe** [dɪ'skraɪb] (v.) 描述
2. **die from** 死於
3. **heart attack** 心臟病
4. **bare** [ber] (a.) 裸露的
5. **wound** [waʊnd] (n.) 傷口
6. **mangled** ['mæŋgəld] (a.) 受嚴重損傷
7. **pass away** 過世
8. **kneel** [niːl] (v.) 跪
9. **barely** ['berli] (adv.) 勉強地
10. **hiss** [hɪs] (v.) 發出嘶嘶聲

Arthur started to lean over, but Van Helsing grabbed him and pulled him back. Lucy suddenly hissed[10] in anger. Her teeth were white and long. Suddenly, her face softened, and she took Arthur's hand in hers.

"My dear, I love you." Then she died.

"Poor girl," I said. "It is the end."

"No, it is only the beginning," whispered Van Helsing.

Why did Lucy want to kiss Arthur?

  [a] She wanted to say goodbye.

  [b] She loved him very much.

  [c] She wanted to bite his neck.

Ans: c

85

A Fill in the blanks with the given words.

> heartbeat   ignorance   bare   spirits

❶ Lucy was in cheerful _____ on the third night Dr. Seward came to watch her.

❷ Van Helsing felt for Lucy's _____ and found it was very feeble.

❸ In her _____, Lucy's mother almost killed her daughter.

❹ Lucy's throat was _____, and they could see two holes in her neck.

B Match.

❶ Mina finds Lucy   •   •   ⓐ at an insane asylum.

❷ Arthur provides shelter for Lucy   •   •   ⓑ in his house.

❸ Van Helsing breaks the window   •   •   ⓒ in the kitchen.

❹ Dr. Seward works   •   •   ⓓ on a tombstone outside the church.

C True or False.

T F ❶ The captain did not have his log book.

T F ❷ Mina left Lucy in Whitby to go see Jonathan in Budapest.

T F ❸ Arthur would not leave Lucy's side while she was sick.

T F ❹ Lucy used to sleepwalk when she was young.

D Choose the correct answer.

❶ What did the townspeople think of the captain of the Demeter?

   (a) They thought he was a madman who killed his crew.

   (b) They thought he was a hero for bringing his ship in.

   (c) They thought he was a vampire.

❷ How did Mina find out what happened to Jonathan in Transylvania?

   (a) She read his journal.

   (b) He told her everything from his hospital bed.

   (c) Dr. Van Helsing told Mina what happened.

· Chapter Five ·

🎧34 The Beautiful Lady

Dr. Seward's story continued

After the funeral for Lucy and her mother, there were odd newspaper articles[1] about children in the neighborhood. Several children had gone missing all night and when they returned home, they talked about a "Beautiful Lady". The police dismissed[2] these stories as children just repeating the excuses of others.

One afternoon, Van Helsing came to my office and thrust[3] last night's "Westminster Gazette" into my hand.

---

1. **article** [ˈɑːrtɪkəl] (n.) 文章
2. **dismiss** [dɪsˈmɪs] (v.) 不受理
3. **thrust** [θrʌst] (v.) 塞（東西）
4. **decoy away** 引誘；誘騙
   decoy [ˈdiːkɔɪ] (v.)
5. **passage** [ˈpæsɪdʒ] (n.)
   一段；一節
6. **puncture** [ˈpʌŋktʃər] (n.) 刺傷
7. **strike** [straɪk] (v.)使突然想起
8. **injure** [ˈɪndʒər] (v.) 傷害
9. **sheer** [ʃɪr] (a.) 全然的
10. **if only** 但願……就好了
11. **hold up** 拿起

"What do you think of that?" he asked as he stood back and folded his arms.

The article was about children being decoyed away[4] at Hampstead. I reached a passage[5] where it described small puncture[6] wounds on their throats. An idea struck[7] me, and I said, "Whatever it was that injured Lucy has injured[8] them."

"I am afraid it's more serious than that," Van Helsing said. "The wounds were made by Lucy herself!"

In sheer[9] anger, I rose up and said, "Dr. Van Helsing, are you mad?"

He looked at me with a pained expression. "If only[10] I were." Then he held up[11] a key. "This is the key to Lucy's tomb. Come with me, and I will show you."

35

That night, we entered the tomb where Lucy lay. But when Van Helsing moved the stone slab[1] over her coffin[2], Lucy's body was not there!

We waited outside the tomb, and soon we saw a figure in white go inside. We followed the figure into the tomb, and once again, Van Helsing moved the stone slab. There lay Lucy, her face white, but with blood red lips! Indeed, a few spots[3] of blood were on her chin! Van Helsing pulled her lip back, and I could see long, white teeth stained[4] with blood.

1. **slab** [slæb] (n.) 厚板；平板
2. **coffin** [ˈkɔːfɪn] (n.) 棺木
3. **spot** [spɑːt] (n.) 點；滴
4. **stain** [steɪn] (v.) 沾污；變髒
5. **victim** [ˈvɪktɪm] (n.) 受害者
6. **feed off** 以……為食物
7. **the undead** 不死之人
8. **curse** [kɜːrs] (n.) 詛咒

Quickly, we left the tomb. I was shaking as Van Helsing explained what had happened.

"Lucy has become the victim[5] of a vampire," he said. "She is feeding off[6] these poor children. Soon, she will be strong enough to kill them. She has become one of the undead[7]. We must free her from this curse[8]. But we will need her fiance, Arthur."

The next day, we met with Arthur. At first, he reacted[9] in much the same way I did, calling Van Helsing a raving[10] lunatic[11]. My long friendship with Arthur enabled me to calm[12] him, and with Van Helsing, we persuaded[13] him to visit Lucy's tomb that night.

✓ *Check Up* True or False.

a Lucy was always in her tomb.　　　　＿＿＿

b Van Helsing needs Arthur's help to
　 free Lucy of her curse.　　　　　　＿＿＿

c Lucy is strong enough to kill the undead.　＿＿＿

Ans: a F b T c F

---

9. **react** [riˈækt] (v.) 反應

10. **raving** [ˈreɪvɪŋ] (a.)
　　胡說八道的

11. **lunatic** [ˈluːnətɪk] (n.) 瘋子

12. **calm** [kɑːlm] (v.) 冷靜

13. **persuade** [pərˈsweɪd] (v.)
　　說服

36

As before, when we opened Lucy's grave, her body was not there. We went outside to wait. Soon after, we saw Lucy arrive. She was carrying a child. When she saw us, she hissed like an angry cat and threw the child to the ground. Suddenly, she walked toward Arthur. She spoke in a soft voice that sounded[1] loving but was hard underneath[2].

"Come, my husband," she said. "Leave them and come rest with me."

Arthur began to move toward her, as if in a trance[3]. I grabbed his arm and held him back. Van Helsing leapt forward and brandished[4] his crucifix. Lucy shrank back. She went to the entrance[5] of the tomb and passed through the closed door!

We followed her inside and found her lying in her grave, as if asleep. Van Helsing handed a hammer and wooden stake[6] to Arthur.

1. **sound** [saʊnd] (v.) 聽起來
2. **underneath** [ˌʌndərˈniːθ] (adv.) 在下面地
3. **trance** [ˌtræns] (n.) 催眠
4. **brandish** [ˈbrændɪʃ] (v.) 揮舞
5. **entrance** [ˈentrəns] (n.) 入口
6. **stake** [steɪk] (n.) 樁；棍子
7. **set free** 解放；解脫
8. **pound** [paʊnd] (v.) 敲擊
9. **stream down** 流下
10. **struggle** [ˈstrʌgəl] (v.) 掙扎
11. **instantly** [ˈɪnstəntli] (adv.) 立刻地；馬上地
12. **limp** [lɪmp] (a.) 無力的

"You must set her free[7]," Van Helsing said. "Drive this stake through her heart the second I begin praying."

As Van Helsing started his prayer, Arthur pounded[8] the stake with the hammer into Lucy's chest. Tears were streaming down[9] his face. Her body moved and struggled[10]. Arthur hit the stake again, and Lucy's body changed instantly[11]. It became limp[12], and her face became peaceful. It was the real Lucy again, not the terrible monster she had become. At last, she was free.

Check Up Short answer question.
How did Lucy escape back into her tomb?

_____

Ans: She passed through the closed door.

93

A Terrible Vampire Lady

In Bram Stoker's novel, Lucy turned into a beautiful vampire lady who preyed on[1] little children. In real life, a noble woman in Hungary closely resembled[2] this description. Her name was Elizabeth Bathory. She was born in 1560 to a very rich and powerful Hungarian family. She had long, black hair against smooth, pale[3] skin. Unfortunately, Elizabeth fell in love with her own beauty.

It is said that one day, as Elizabeth was older, a servant[4] girl pulled Elizabeth's hair while brushing[5] it. Elizabeth slapped[6] the girl's hand so hard that one of her rings caused the girl to bleed[7]. When the blood touched Elizabeth's skin, it made a red, youthful[8] glow[9].

1. **prey on** 捕食
2. **resemble** [rɪˈzembəl] (v.) 類似
3. **pale** [peɪl] (a.) 蒼白的
4. **servant** [ˈsɜːrvənt] (n.) 僕人
5. **brush** [brʌʃ] (v.) 梳
6. **slap** [slæp] (v.) 打；擊
7. **bleed** [bliːd] (v.) 流血
8. **youthful** [ˈjuːθfəl] (a.) 年輕的

Elizabeth was very interested in trying to stay young. She thought that by using blood, she could stay beautiful. So she and her servants began capturing[10] young girls in the area. They would torture[11] them, kill them, and take all of their blood. When peasants[12] found the bloodless[13] bodies outside the castle, rumors were started that Elizabeth was a vampire.

Finally, the Prime Minister of Hungary, who was Elizabeth's cousin, came to her castle. He found the dead bodies of young girls, and even some girls who were waiting to be killed.

Local legends say that her ghost[14] still roams the Carpathian mountains near her castle.

---

9. **glow** [gloʊ] (n.) 光輝；灼熱
10. **capture** [ˈkæptʃər] (v.) 捕捉
11. **torture** [ˈtɔːrtʃər] (v.) 虐待

12. **peasant** [ˈpɛzənt] (n.) 農人
13. **bloodless** [ˈblʌdləs] (a.) 無血的
14. **ghost** [goʊst] (n.) 鬼魂

Chapter Six

🎧37 The Hunt for Dracula

After Lucy's funeral, Mina contacted Van Helsing because he seemed to know much about her friend's death. After Mina heard the strange tale, she gave Jonathan's diary to him. This is how Van Helsing learned about Count Dracula and his arrival in England.

After the vampire Lucy was killed, Van Helsing called Dr. Seward, Arthur, Jonathan, and Mina together for a meeting.

"We must destroy Count Dracula," he said. "He is a very strong vampire. When he forces[1] someone to drink his blood, they become his slave[2]. He is as strong as twenty men. He is very intelligent, and he can change his shape into that of a wolf, a bat, or even a fine[3] mist[4] that can move through the tiniest[5] cracks[6]. But he has some weaknesses. He can only move around during the night. During the daylight hours, he is confined to[7] his coffin like the truly dead."

Then Van Helsing turned to Jonathan.

"You say he left his castle in Transylvania with 50 great boxes?"

Jonathan nodded[8].

1. **force** [fɔːrs] (v.) 強迫
2. **slave** [sleɪv] (n.) 奴隸
3. **fine** [faɪn] (a.) 細微的
4. **mist** [mɪst] (n.) 薄霧
5. **tiny** ['taɪni] (a.) 細小的
6. **crack** [kræk] (n.) 裂口
7. **be confined to**
   受限於；拘束於
8. **nod** [nɑːd] (v.) 點頭
   (nod-nodded-nodded)

38 "Then we must find all of these boxes and destroy them," continued Van Helsing. "Then he will have nowhere to rest and will become weak. He may even die."

The obvious[1] place to search was Carfax, the estate Jonathan helped the Count to buy. The men found it was more like an old castle than a mansion[2], with dank[3], smelly[4] tunnels underneath. It was in these tunnels that the vampire hunters found Dracula's boxes.

They opened each and Van Helsing sprinkled[5] holy water in every one. As he did this, he said a prayer. Finally, he put a sacred[6] wafer[7], the same ones that are used in church to symbolize[8] Christ's body, in each coffin. Before he got to the last one however, the men heard something moving toward them.

"We are too late," cried Van Helsing. "Count Dracula has returned!"

The men spread out ready to attack, but they trembled[9] at the sight of the Count as he entered the room. He moved with a supernatural[10] quickness[11]. Van Helsing held up his crucifix and the Count backed away[12]. That gave the men the opportunity[13] to run outside.

"Quick," said Van Helsing. "He knows we are on his trail[14]. He may try to strike at your house, Jonathan! Mina is in danger!"

✓ Check Up

What is Van Helsing's plan to destroy Count Dracula?

  a He plans to throw holy water on him.

  b He wants to destroy all of his resting boxes.

  c He will try to surround Count Dracula with crucifixes.

Ans: b

---

1. **obvious** [ˈɑːbviəs] (a.) 明顯的

2. **mansion** [ˈmænʃən] (n.) 豪宅

3. **dank** [dæŋk] (a.) 潮濕的

4. **smelly** [ˈsmeli] (a.) 難聞的

5. **sprinkle** [ˈsprɪŋkəl] (v.) 撒；潑

6. **sacred** [ˈseɪkrɪd] (a.) 神聖的

7. **wafer** [ˈweɪfər] (n.) （天主教做彌撒用的）聖餅

8. **symbolize** [ˈsɪmbəlaɪz] (v.) 象徵

9. **tremble** [ˈtrembəl] (v.) 發抖

10. **supernatural** [ˌsuːpərˈnætʃərəl] (a.) 超乎自然的

11. **quickness** [ˈkwɪknɪs] (n.) 敏捷；快速

12. **back away** 後退

13. **opportunity** [ˌɑːpərˈtuːnəti] (n.) 機會

14. **on one's trail** 追蹤；跟蹤

39

They all rushed back to Jonathan's house, and ran upstairs to Mina's bedroom. The door was locked which Jonathan remarked[1] was unusual. The men broke the door open and a terrible sight met their eyes. There was Mina, in her white sleeping clothes, standing limply upright[2] next to her bed. By her side stood a tall, thin man, clad[3] in black. His face was turned from the men, but the instant they saw him, they all recognized[4] the Count.

With his left hand he held both Mrs. Harker's hands, keeping them away with her arms fully stretched[5] above her. His right hand gripped her by the back of the neck, forcing her face down on his bosom[6]. Her white night-dress was smeared[7] with blood, and a thin stream trickled down[8] the man's bare chest, which was shown by his torn-open[9] shirt.

---

1. **remark** [rɪˈmɑːrk] (v.) 說
2. **upright** [ˈʌpraɪt] (adv.) 垂直地;直立地
3. **clad** [klæd] (a.) 穿著……的
4. **recognize** [ˈrekəgnaɪz] (v.) 辨認
5. **stretch** [stretʃ] (v.) 伸展
6. **bosom** [ˈbʊzəm] (n.) 胸
7. **smear** [smɪr] (v.) 弄髒;沾汙
8. **trickle down** 流下
9. **torn-open** [ˈtɔːrnˈoʊpən] (a.) 撕開的
10. **hellish** [ˈhelɪʃ] (a.) 兇惡的
11. **devilish** [ˈdevəlɪʃ] (a.) 惡魔般的
12. **spring at** 跳躍
13. **fixed** [fɪkst] (a.) 固定不動的
14. **chant** [tʃænt] (v.) 吟唱
15. **cower back** 退縮;畏縮

As the men burst into the room, the Count turned his face, and a hellish[10] look seemed to leap into it. His eyes flamed red with devilish[11] passion. Violently, he threw his victim back upon the bed, and then he turned and sprang at[12] his hunters.

But by this time, the professor was holding his crucifix with a fixed[13] arm and chanting[14] a prayer. The Count suddenly stopped, just as poor Lucy had done outside her tomb, and he cowered back[15].

✓ Check Up

How did Van Helsing stop Dracula's attack?

  a He threw garlic at him.

  b He shot a pistol at him.

  c He held up a crucifix and said a prayer.

Ans: c

40

"Ha!" he yelled. "You think you have defeated[1] me. You know not that I have lived for centuries, and I will live long after your bones have turned to dust[2]. And now the women you love will become mine!"

With that, he vanished in the shadows of the night.

"We must watch over her better than we watched over Lucy," said Van Helsing.

"Tomorrow, we will go back to Carfax and destroy the Count's last box."

Breakfast the next day was a strange affair[3]. They all tried to be cheerful and encourage[4] each other, and Mina was the brightest and most cheerful of all.

When it was over, Van Helsing stood up and said, "Now, my dear friends, we go forth[5] to finish our terrible task[6]. Are we all armed[7], as we were on that night when first we visited our enemy's lair[8]?

---

1. **defeat** [dɪˈfiːt] (v.) 擊敗
2. **dust** [dʌst] (n.) 塵土
3. **affair** [əˈfer] (n.) 場合
4. **encourage** [ɪnˈkɜːrɪdʒ] (v.) 鼓勵
5. **go forth** 前往
6. **task** [tæsk] (n.) 任務；工作
7. **arm** [ɑːrm] (v.) 武裝
8. **lair** [ler] (n.) 庇護所
9. **assure** [əˈʃʊr] (v.) 確認
10. **guard** [gɑːrd] (v.) 保護
11. **in the name of** 以……之名
12. **flesh** [fleʃ] (n.) 肉體

The other men all assured[9] him that they were. "Then it is well. Now, Madam Mina, you are in any case quite safe here until the sunset. But before we go, let me prepare you against personal attack. I have myself, since you came down, prepared your bedroom by the placing of garlic, holy water and sacred wafer, so that he may not enter. Now let me guard[10] you. On your forehead I touch this piece of sacred wafer in the name of[11] the Father, the Son, and . . ."

There was a fearful scream from Mina as soon as he placed the wafer on her forehead. The thin wafer burned into the flesh[12] as though it was a piece of white hot metal.

 Check Up

When Van Helsing put the holy wafer on Mina's forehead, _____ .

a it melted into water
b nothing at all happened
c it burned her skin

Ans: c

41

Van Helsing seemed quite dejected[1].

"Dear Mina, please forgive me," he said.

Then with a grim expression[2] he turned to the others. "Let us go and destroy this monster's last refuge[3] while the sun shines."

While Jonathan watched over Mina, the other men returned to Carfax. However, they could not find the last box.

Returning to Mina's room, Van Helsing said, "Mina has a special connection[4] to the Count now that she has drunk his blood. She can experience what Dracula is experiencing now, and vice versa[5]."

Van Helsing hypnotized[6] Mina. "What can you see?" he asked. "What can you hear? What can you smell?"

Mina spoke slowly, with her eyes closed. "Everything is black and stuffy, like the inside of a box. I can smell the ocean. I can hear the sound of waves and of a ship being made ready to sail."

1. **dejected** [dɪ'dʒɪktɪd] (a.) 沮喪的
2. **expression** [ɪk'spreʃən] (n.) 表情
3. **refuge** ['refjuːdʒ] (n.) 藏身處
4. **connection** [kə'nekʃən] (n.) 連結
5. **vice versa** 反之亦然
6. **hypnotize** ['hɪpnətaɪz] (v.) 催眠
7. **succeed in** 成功地做到
8. **soundly** ['saʊndli] (adv.) 沉穩地；祥和地

"That's it!" cried Jonathan. "He's returning to Transylvania! We have succeeded in[7] driving him away from London!"

"Yes, that is true," replied Van Helsing. "But for Mina's sake, we must follow him and destroy him. If we are too late, Mina will suffer the same fate as Lucy."

It was decided that Van Helsing and Mina would travel together over land to Dracula's castle. Jonathan, Dr. Seward, and Arthur got passage on a fast ship to follow Dracula over the seas. Van Helsing and Mina arrived at Count Dracula's castle well before both the Count and their friends.

It was very cold, and Van Helsing was worried about Mina. She would not sleep during the night; instead, she sat in a sort of trance. And during the day, she slept so soundly[8] that Van Helsing could not wake her. Only during the brief sunrise and sunset would she act like her normal self.

This is what Mina wrote in her diary:

In the late afternoon, I woke up.
The professor signalled[1] to me, so I got up and
joined[2] him. He had found a wonderful spot,
a sort of natural hollow[3] in a rock, with an
entrance like a doorway between two
boulders[4]. He took me by the hand and drew
me in.

"See!" he said, "here you will be sheltered[5].
And if the wolves come, I can meet them one
at a time."

He brought in our furs[6], made a snug[7] nest for me, and tried to offer me some food. But even trying to put food near my mouth was repulsive[8] to me. I wanted to please him, but I could not bring myself to even attempt[9] to eat. He looked very sad but did not scold[10] me. Taking his telescope[11] from the case, he stood on the top of the rock and began to search the horizon[12].

Suddenly he called out, "Look! Madam Mina, look! Look!"

I sprang up and stood beside him on the rock. He handed[13] me his glass and pointed. The snow was now falling more heavily and swirled[14] about fiercely[15], for a high wind was beginning to blow. From the height where we were, it was possible to see a great distance.

1. **signal** ['sɪgnəl] (v.) 以（動作）示意
2. **join** [dʒɔɪn] (v.) 加入
3. **hollow** ['hɑːləʊ] (n.) 洞
4. **boulder** ['boʊldər] (n.) 大圓石
5. **shelter** ['ʃeltər] (v.) 躲避
6. **fur** [fɜːr] (n.) 皮毛
7. **snug** [snʌg] (a.) 舒適的
8. **repulsive** [rɪ'pʌlsɪv] (a.) 令人反感的；厭惡的
9. **attempt** [ə'tempt] (v.) 試圖
10. **scold** [skoʊld] (v.) 責罵
11. **telescope** ['telɪskoʊp] (n.) 望遠鏡
12. **horizon** [hə'raɪzən] (n.) 地平線
13. **hand** [hænd] (v.) 給
14. **swirl** [swɜːrl] (v.) 打旋
15. **fiercely** ['fɪrsli] (adv.) 猛烈地

Straight in front of us and not far off[1] came a group of mounted[2] men hurrying along. In the midst of[3] them was a long wagon which swayed[4] from side to side[5], like a dog's tail wagging[6]. I could see from the men's clothes that they were peasants[7] or Gypsies of some kind.

On the wagon was a great square chest[8]. My heart leapt as I saw it, for I felt that the end was coming. The evening was now drawing close, and I knew that at sunset the thing, which was inside that box would be free.

In fear I turned to the professor. To my surprise[9], however, he was not there. An instant later, I saw him below me. He was drawing a holy[10] circle[11] in the ground around my position and sealing[12] it with a prayer.

When he finished, he stood beside me and said, "At least you shall be safe here from him!"

---

1. **far off** 遙遠的
2. **mounted** [ˈmaʊntɪd] (a.) 騎馬的
3. **in the midst of** 在……中間
4. **sway** [sweɪ] (v.) 搖晃；搖擺
5. **from side to side** 左右來回地
6. **wag** [wæg] (v.) 搖晃
7. **peasant** [ˈpezənt] (n.) 鄉下人；農夫
8. **chest** [tʃest] (n.) 箱子
9. **to one's surprise** 出乎意外地
10. **holy** [ˈhoʊli] (a.) 神聖的
11. **circle** [ˈsɜːrkəl] (n.) 圓圈
12. **seal** [siːl] (v.) 密封
13. **gallop** [ˈɡæləp] (v.) 飛馳
14. **pause** [pɔːz] (v.) 暫停

He took the glass from me and said, "See, they come quickly. They are whipping the horses and galloping[13] as hard as they can."

He paused[14] and went on in a hollow voice, "They are racing for the sunset. We may be too late!"

Then he cried, "Look! Look! Look! See, two horsemen follow fast, coming up from the south. It must be Arthur and John!"

I took the telescope and looked. The two men might have been Dr. Seward and Mr. Holmwood.

✓ *Check Up* Short answer question.
What was in the box on the wagon?

_____

Ans: Count Dracula

In any case, I knew that neither of them was Jonathan. However, somehow[1], I knew that Jonathan was not far off. Looking around, I saw on the north side of the coming party two other men riding at breakneck[2] speed. I knew one of them was Jonathan, and the other was Lord Godalming, Arthur's friend from London who so graciously[3] came with us on our dangerous hunt. They, too, were pursuing[4] the party with the cart. When I told the professor, he shouted in glee[5] like a schoolboy, and then he laid his Winchester rifle[6] ready for use against the rock.

1. **somehow** [ˈsʌmhaʊ] (adv.) 不知怎麼地

2. **breakneck** [ˈbreɪknek] (a.) 極快的

3. **graciously** [ˈɡreɪʃəsli] (adv.) 慷慨地；仁慈地

4. **pursue** [pərˈsuː] (v.) 追趕

5. **in glee** 欣喜地

6. **rifle** [ˈraɪfəl] (n.) 來福槍

7. **converge** [kənˈvɜːrdʒ] (v.) 聚集

8. **revolver** [rɪˈvɑːlvər] (n.) 左輪手槍

9. **howling** [ˈhaʊlɪŋ] (n.) 咆哮

10. **prey** [preɪ] (n.) 捕食

11. **burst** [bɜːrst] (n.) 爆發；爆裂

12. **accuracy** [ˈækʊrəsi] (n.) 準確性；精確

"They are all converging[7]," he said. "When the time comes, we shall have the gypsies from all sides."

I got out my revolver[8], for while we were speaking, the howling[9] of wolves came louder and closer. The wolves were gathering for their prey[10].

Every instant seemed an age while we waited. The wind came now in fierce bursts[11], and the snow was driven with fury, yet the sun still shone here and there. We were accustomed to watching for sunrise and sunset, so we knew with fair accuracy[12] that the sun would soon set.

☑ Check Up

Van Helsing and Mina worried _____ .

a that the snow will help Dracula escape

b that Jonathan is not there

c that the sun will soon set

Ans: c

Soon, we could clearly distinguish[1] the individuals[2] of each party, the hunted and the hunters. Strangely enough, the Gypsies did not seem to realize, or perhaps they didn't care, that they were being pursued. They seemed, however, to double their speed as the sun dropped lower and lower on the mountain tops.

All at once[3] two voices shouted out, "Halt!"

One was my Jonathan's, the other Mr. Holmwood's strong, resolute[4] tone of command. The Gypsies may not have known the language, but there was no mistaking intent[5]. Instinctively[6], they pulled their horses to a stop.

Lord Godalming and Jonathan dashed[7] up to one side, and Dr. Seward and Mr. Holmwood went to the other. The leader of the Gypsies waved them back, and in a fierce[8] voice told his companions[9] to proceed[10].

They lashed the horses and sprang forward. But the four men raised their Winchester rifles, and at the same moment, Dr. Van Helsing and I rose from behind the rock and pointed our weapons[11] at them. Seeing that they were surrounded, the Gypsies gathered together. Their leader turned to them and said something at which every Gypsy drew whatever weapon he carried, knife or pistol, and they held themselves in readiness to attack.

1. **distinguish** [dɪ'stɪŋgwɪʃ] (v.) 分辨；辨別
2. **individual** [ˌɪndɪ'vɪdʒuəl] (n.) 個體；個人
3. **all at once** 突然
4. **resolute** ['rezəluːt] (a.) 堅決的；果敢的
5. **intent** [ɪn'tent] (n.) 意圖
6. **instinctively** [ɪn'stɪŋktɪvli] (adv.) 出於本能的；直覺的
7. **dash** [dæʃ] (v.) 衝
8. **fierce** [fɪrs] (a.) 猛烈的
9. **companion** [kəm'pænjən] (n.) 夥伴；朋友
10. **proceed** [prə'siːd] (v.) 前進
11. **weapon** ['wepən] (n.) 武器

✓ Check Up

Why did the Gypsies increase their speed?

a̲ They wanted to reach their destination before the storm got worse.

b̲ They wanted to cscape their pursuers.

c̲ They wanted to get to where they were going before the sun set.

46

The Gypsy leader pointed first to the sun, now close near the mountain peaks[1], and then to the castle. He said something which I did not understand. As if in answer, all four men of our party threw themselves from their horses and dashed toward the cart.

Strangely, I felt no fear, but only a wild desire to do something. Seeing the quick movement of our men the leader of the Gypsies gave a command. His men instantly formed a circle round the cart.

I could see Jonathan on one side of the ring of men and Arthur on the other. They were forcing a way to the cart. It was clear that they were bent on[2] finishing their task before the sun could set. Nothing seemed to stop or even to hinder[3] them.

Neither the levelled[4] weapons nor the flashing[5] knives of the gypsies in front, nor the howling of the wolves behind, appeared to even attract their attention[6]. Jonathan's grim face and singleness[7] of purpose seemed to overawe[8] the Gypsies in front of him.

---

1. **peak** [piːk] (n.) 頂峰
2. **be bent on** 下決心
3. **hinder** [ˈhɪndər] (v.) 阻礙
4. **levelled** [ˈlevəld] (a.) 對準的
5. **flashing** [ˈflæʃɪŋ] (a.)閃光的

Instinctively, they cowered aside and let him pass. In an instant, he jumped upon the cart, and with a strength which seemed incredible[9], pushed the great box over the side to the ground.

6. **attract one's attention**
   吸引注意

7. **singleness** [ˈsɪŋɡəlnɪs]
   (n.) 專注

8. **overawe** [ˌoʊvərˈɔː] (v.)
   嚇倒

9. **incredible** [ɪnˈkrɛdɪbəl]
   (a.) 不可思議的

47

In the meantime, Arthur pushed desperately[1] forward, as the Gypsies cut at him with their flashing knives. He parried[2] them with his great bowie[3] knife, and at first I thought that he too had come through in safety. But as he sprang beside Jonathan, who had by now jumped from the cart, I could see that with his left hand he was clutching[4] at his side, and blood was spurting[5] through his fingers.

He did not delay, however, and through the efforts of both men the lid[6] of the box began to yield[7]. The nails drew with a screeching[8] sound, and the top of the box was thrown back.

By this time the gypsies, seeing themselves covered by the rifles of Lord Godalming, Dr. Seward, and Van Helsing, had given in[9] and made no further resistance[10].

---

1. **desperately** [ˈdespərɪtli] (adv.) 不顧一切地
2. **parry** [ˈpæri] (v.) 擋開；迴避
3. **bowie** [ˈboʊi] (n.) 波伊刀（一種鋼製獵刀）
4. **clutch** [klʌtʃ] (v.) 抓著
5. **spurt** [spɜːrt] (v.) 噴出
6. **lid** [lɪd] (n.) 蓋子
7. **yield** [jiːld] (v.) 垮掉
8. **screeching** [ˈskriːtʃɪŋ] (a.) 刺耳的

9. **give in** 讓步
10. **resistance** [rɪˈzɪstəns] (n.) 抵抗
11. **deathly** [ˈdeθli] (a.) 像死了的
12. **vindictive** [vɪnˈdɪktɪv] (a.) 惡意的；憎恨的
13. **triumph** [ˈtraɪəmf] (n.) 勝利
14. **sweep** [swiːp] (n.) 揮；掃過
15. **shriek** [ʃriːk] (v.) 尖叫
16. **shear** [ʃɪr] (v.) 砍
17. **plunge** [plʌndʒ] (v.) 刺進
    plunge into 刺進

The sun was almost down on the mountain tops. I saw the Count lying within the box upon his earth. He was deathly[11] pale, and his red eyes glared with the horrible vindictive[12] look which I knew so well. As I looked, his eyes saw the sinking sun, and the look of hate in them turned to triumph[13].

But, in the instant, came the sweep[14] and flash of Jonathan's great knife. I shrieked[15] as I saw it shear[16] through his throat. At the same moment, Arthur's bowie knife plunged into[17] his heart.

✓ Check Up

What happened to Arthur?

- a He was shot by one of the Gypsies.
- b One of the Gypsies cut him with a knife.
- c He was knocked over by one of the Gypsies' horses.

48

It was like a miracle[1], but before our very eyes, the whole body crumbled[2] into dust and passed from our sight. I shall be glad as long as I live that even in that moment, there was in Dracula's face a look of peace, such as I never could have imagined might have rested there.

The Gypsies turned, and without a word, rode away as if for their lives. Those who were on foot jumped upon the wagon and shouted to the horsemen not to desert[3] them. The wolves followed behind them, leaving us alone.

Arthur sank to the ground and, leaning on his elbow, held his hand pressed to his side. The blood still gushed[4] through his fingers. I ran to him, as did the two doctors. Jonathan knelt behind him. With a sigh, Arthur feebly took my hand in his unstained[5] hand.

1. **miracle** [ˈmɪrɪkəl] (n.) 奇蹟
2. **crumble** [ˈkrʌmbəl] (v.) 粉碎；破裂
3. **desert** [dɪˈzɜːrt] (v.) 拋棄
4. **gush** [gʌʃ] (v.) 噴；湧
5. **unstained** [ʌnˈsteɪnd] (a.) 未污染的
6. **anguish** [ˈæŋgwɪʃ] (n.) 苦惱
7. **be of service** 有幫助的
8. **posture** [ˈpɔːstʃər] (n.) 姿勢
9. **gleam** [gliːm] (n.) 微光
10. **fall upon** 落在⋯⋯上
11. **impulse** [ˈɪmpʌls] (n.) 衝動
12. **earnest** [ˈɜːrnɪst] (a.) 誠懇的
13. **grief** [griːf] (n.) 悲傷
14. **in silence** 沉默地
15. **gallant** [ˈgælənt] (a.) 英勇的

He must have seen the anguish[6] of my heart in my face, for he smiled at me and said, "I am only too happy to have been of service[7]! Oh, God!" he cried suddenly, struggling to a sitting posture[8] and pointing to me. "It was worth it for me to die! Look! Look!"

The sun was now right down upon the mountain top, and the red gleams[9] fell upon[10] my face, so that it was bathed in rosy light. With one impulse[11], the men sank on their knees. From their lips came a deep and earnest[12] "Amen" as they saw that the red mark that had been burned into my forehead was now gone!

Arthur said, "Now God be thanked that all has not been in vain! See! The curse has passed away!"

And, to our bitter grief[13], with a smile and in silence[14], he died, a gallant[15] gentleman.

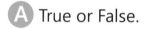 True or False.

T F ❶ The children were calling Lucy "The Beautiful Lady."

T F ❷ When Van Helsing and Dr. Seward first looked in Lucy's coffin, her body was there.

T F ❸ Dracula made Mina drink his blood.

T F ❹ Van Helsing wanted to wound Mina with the Sacred Wafer.

T F ❺ Count Dracula's boxes were in the basement of the Carfax castle.

T F ❻ Van Helsing shot the Gypsies with his rifle.

Ⓑ Rearrange the sentences in chronological order.

❶ Children begin to go missing at night.

❷ Van Helsing tells Arthur that Lucy has become a vampire.

❸ Lucy tries to charm Arthur into joining her.

❹ Van Helsing visits Dr. Seward in his office.

❺ Lucy throws the child to the ground.

_____ ⇨ _____ ⇨ _____ ⇨ _____ ⇨ _____

C Choose the correct answer.

❶ Why did Dr. Seward become angry with Van Helsing?

(a) The bill for Van Helsing's services was much too high.

(b) Van Helsing accused Lucy of something terrible.

(c) Van Helsing called Dr. Seward an idiot.

❷ How was Lucy the vampire killed?

(a) Van Helsing hit her on the head with his crucifix.

(b) Dr. Seward cut her head off.

(c) Arthur hammered a wooden stake through her heart.

❸ How did Arthur become fatally wounded?

(a) The Gypsies stabbed Arthur with a knife.

(b) The Gypsies shot Arthur with their guns.

(c) Count Dracula threw Arthur onto some rocks.

❹ Why did Dracula leave England?

(a) He was afraid of Jonathan.

(b) Almost all of his boxes were destroyed.

(c) He wanted Mina to follow him to Translyvania.

Appendixes

Guide to Listening Comprehension

When listening to the story, use some of the techniques shown below. If you take time to study some phonetic characteristics of English, listening will be easier.

Get in the flow of English.

English creates a rhythm formed by combinations of strong and weak stress intonations. Each word has its particular stress that combines with other words to form the overall pattern of stress or rhythm in a particular sentence.

When you are speaking and listening to English, it is essential to get in the flow of the rhythm of English. It takes a lot of practice to get used to such a rhythm. So, you need to start by identifying the stressed syllable in a word.

Listen for the strongly stressed words and phrases.

In English, key words and phrases that are essential to the meaning of a sentence are stressed louder. Therefore, pay attention to the words stressed with a higher pitch. When listening to an English recording for the first time, what matters most is to listen for a general understanding of what you hear. Do not try to hear every single word. Most of the unstressed words are articles or auxiliary verbs, which don't play an important role in the general context. At this level, you can ignore them.

Pay attention to liaisons.

In reading English, words are written with a space between them. There isn't such an obvious guide when it comes to listening to English. In oral English, there are many cases when the sounds of words are linked with adjacent words.

For instance, let's think about the phrase "**take off**," which can be used in "take off your clothes." "Take off your clothes" doesn't sound like [teɪk ɔːf] with each of the words completely and clearly separated from the others. Instead, it sounds as if almost all the words in context are slurred together, [ˌteɪkɔːf], for a more natural sound.

Shadow the voice of the native speaker.

Finally, you need to mimic the voice of the native speaker. Once you are sure you know how to pronounce all the words in a sentence, try to repeat them like an echo. Listen to the book again, but this time you should try a fun exercise while listening to the English.

This exercise is called "shadowing." The word "shadow" means a dark shade that is formed on a surface. When used as a verb, the word refers to the action of following someone or something like a shadow. In this exercise, pretend you are a parrot and try to shadow the voice of the native speaker.

Try to mimic the reader's voice by speaking at the same speed, with the same strong and weak stresses on words, and pausing or stopping at the same points.

Experts have already proven this technique to be effective. If you practice this shadowing exercise, your English speaking and listening skills will improve by leaps and bounds. While shadowing the native speaker, don't forget to pay attention to the meaning of each phrase and sentence.

Listen to what you want to shadow many times. Start out by just trying to shadow a few words or a sentence.

 Mimic the CD out loud. You can shadow everything the speaker says as if you are singing a round, or you also can speak simultaneously with the recorded voice of the native speaker.

 As you practice more, try to shadow more. For instance, shadow a whole sentence or paragraph instead of just a few words.

Listening Guide

Chapter One page 14–15 🎧49

In early 1897, the London lawyer Jonathan Harker traveled from London to Transylvania to meet a client named Count Dracula. Harker (❶) ( ) real estate; the count (❷) ( ) buy some property in London. This is Harker's journal:

3 May

Count Dracula told me to stay at the Golden Krone Hotel in Bistritz. This is a scenic town in the shadow of the Carpathian Mountains. (❸) ( ) ( ) I arrived, the innkeeper's wife gave me a (❺).

It read, "My Friend. Welcome to the Carpathians. Sleep well tonight. At three tomorrow afternoon, a coach will leave for the town of Bukovina. I have reserved a seat for you. When you (❺) ( ) Borgo Pass, you will meet my driver, who will bring you to me.

Your friend, Dracula"

以下為《吸血鬼》各章節的前半部。一開始若能聽清楚發音，之後就沒有聽力的負擔。先聽過摘錄的章節，之後再反覆聆聽括弧內單字的發音，並仔細閱讀各種發音的説明。以下都是以英語的典型發音為基礎所做的簡易説明，即使這裡未提到的發音，也可以配合音檔反覆聆聽，如此一來聽力必能更上層樓。

❶ worked in：當這兩個單字連續唸時，worked 結尾的無聲子音 [t]，會和 in 開頭的母音 [ɪ] 結合，變化成 [tɪn] 的發音。

❷ wanted to：這兩個字連在一起時，由於 wanted 的字尾為 d，而 to 的字首為 t，d 與 t 的發音接近，且 t 是字首，故而在讀音時，wanted 的 d 要退居幕後，含在口中與 t 混和，聽起來只有 t 的聲音。

❸ As soon as：由於 As 的字尾和 soon 的字首皆為 s，因此可連音；soon 的字尾和 as 的字首為子母音連音，全句發為 [əsuːnəz]。

❹ letter：這個字不論前後接什麼字，在美語中它的讀音都要輕巧。因為它雖然有兩個 t，卻只發一個 t，而 t 是吐氣音。

❺ get to：由於 get 的字尾為 t，而 to 的字首也為 t，因此唸起來就像 geto。

4 May

When I (❶) (   ) innkeeper about the Count, he acted strangely. Before, he understood my (❷) German well. But when I asked about Dracula, he told me he didn't understand. He and his wife gave each other (❸) looks. Finally, after I kept asking, they told me that they knew nothing. Then they (❹) (   ) sign of the cross. This was all very odd.

Just as I had finished packing my suitcase for the trip, the old lady nervously came into my room. "Young Herr, do you really have to go?" she asked. I replied I had to go, as it was business. She asked me if I really knew where and what I was going to do. Finally, she got on her knees and begged me not to go.

"What silliness," I thought. I helped her (❺) (   ) and told her firmly that it was my business to go, and nothing could interfere with that. She wiped tears from her eyes. Then she took off the crucifix that hung (❻) (   ) neck and put it around my neck.

"For your mother's sake," she said before leaving my room.

1 **asked the**：過去式 -ed 前面若是為 [p]、[k]、[f]、[s] 等無聲子音，會發 [t] 音。

2 **basic**：basic 的重音在第一音節，這個字不論前後接什麼字，在美語中它的讀音都要輕巧。

3 **frightened**：這個字要注意 en 的 e 不發音。ten 的發音是 [tn]，讀音時 t 含在口中，不把氣音吐出，而與 n 合在一起。這樣的發音例子不少，如 cotton、gotten、bitten，但是一般往往因為 [tn] 發音不易，或以為 e 要發音，而把它讀成 [tən]。

4 **made the**：made 與 the 連在一起發音時，made 的 [d] 音與 the 的 [ð] 音會產生連音。

5 **stand up**：當無聲子音 [s] 和 [t] 連唸時，[t] 會變化成有聲子音 [d]，成為 [sd] 的發音。

6 **around her**：在英語的會話中，常常可以見到 h 的音消失的情形。h 的音消失後，就只剩下 -er 和前面的 around，因此合起來就變成 arounder。通常以 h 開頭的代名詞（he、him、his、her 等）和助動詞（have、had 等）依前後文迅速發弱音時，[h] 音會略過聽不清楚。

3

Listening Comprehension

 A Listen to the CD and write down the sentences and names.

| Count Dracula | Jonathan | Van Helsing | Lucy | Arthur Holmwood |

❶ _____ _____

❷ _____ _____

❸ _____ _____

❹ _____ _____

❺ _____ _____

B Listen to the CD and fill in the blanks.

❶ When I _____ the innkeeper _____ the Count, he acted strangely.

❷ She _____ tears from her _____.

❸ His English was _____, but he spoke with a strange _____.

❹ As soon as he _____, I must _____ for Budapest.

❺ This schedule began to _____ its _____ on me.

C Listen to the CD, write down the question and choose the correct answer.

❶ _____?

    (a) a group of Russian peasants

    (b) a band of gypsies

    (c) a pack of wolves

❷ _____?

    (a) Transylvania

    (b) London

    (c) Budapest

D Listen to the CD. True or False.

T F ❶ ....

T F ❷ ....

T F ❸ ....

T F ❹ ....

伯蘭‧史杜克（Bram Stoker, 1847–1912）

伯蘭‧史杜克 1847 年 11 月 8 日出生於愛爾蘭都柏林。童年時期身體孱弱，常常臥病在床。青少年的他喜好閱讀寫作，儘管父親強烈反對，他仍希望有朝一日能成為作家。自都柏林大學畢業後，他成為公務員。

在任職期間，史杜克運用空閒時光擔任劇評家與雜誌編輯。不久，他認識了演員亨利‧艾爾文（Henry Irving），兩人建立起終身不渝的友誼，這份關係也似乎對史杜克整個職業生涯產生巨大影響。

1878 年，史杜克與佛羅倫斯‧博肯（Florence Balcombe）結婚，之前身兼作家、詩人與劇評家的王爾德（Oscar Wilde）也曾追求過她。之後史杜克辭去八年的公務員工作搬到倫敦，在亨利‧艾爾文擁有的萊塞姆劇院（Lyceum Theater）擔任劇院經理。

史杜克一邊認真完成工作一邊當個作家。除了他 1879 年出版的第一本書 *Duties of Clerks of Petty Sessions in Ireland*，他也有許多長篇與短篇的著作出版。1897 年，史杜克的哥德式驚悚小説《吸血鬼》替他贏得舉世名聲。他是個真誠不懈的作家，全心奉獻於寫作中，直到於 1912 年 4 月 20 日辭世。

　　故事一開始，英國人強納森‧哈克啟程去拜訪住在羅馬尼亞外西凡尼亞的德古拉伯爵。德古拉假借於倫敦置產之名，輕易地將哈克騙上門。

　　德古拉其實是個以活人鮮血維生的吸血鬼，他與三位女吸血鬼已經在古堡裡存活了好幾個世紀。留宿古堡期間，哈克飽受恐懼與懷疑的折騰。他漸漸地發現自己受德古拉監禁，於是睹上性命採取了關鍵行動逃離古堡。

　　這期間，哈克的未婚妻米娜與朋友露西同住。然而，露西突然開始在晚上離家外出，因好友日漸蒼白的臉色與怪異的行為舉止，米娜逐漸擔憂起來……

　　《吸血鬼》是伯蘭‧史杜克的傑作，曾無數次登上舞台與大銀幕，每次都為讀者帶來興奮驚悚的震撼，有時也讓讀者恐懼得整夜無法成眠。

p. 12–13 **人物簡介**

Dracula 德古拉伯爵

　　好幾世紀以來，我都住在外西凡尼亞城堡的黑暗世界裡。四周的村民們都認識我，而且很怕我。我應該要搬到一個沒有人認識我的新地方了。為此，我派人找了一個來自倫敦的年輕房地產律師。他會幫我籌備搬家事宜，但是，他將永遠都無法離開我的城堡。哈！哈！

Jonathan Harker 強納生・哈克

　　我是個房地產界的年輕律師。老闆派我去外西凡尼亞服務一個叫德古拉伯爵的有錢客戶。這位伯爵想要在倫敦置產，而且他的需求非常特殊。我必須離開我美麗的未婚妻米娜去處理這筆生意。這幾週忙完後，我們就要結婚了。

Mina 米娜

　　我親愛的強納生被派到一個我未曾聽聞的陌生國家出差。我真希望他能平安。當他回來時，我們就要結婚了。而現在，我要幫我最好的朋友露西籌備她和一個優秀的英國紳士的婚禮。

Arthur Holmwood 亞瑟・霍伍德

　　我是個有錢的英國紳士，在倫敦也有置產。不久後，我就要跟一個名叫露西的年輕女孩結婚了，但是她卻病得很重。我願不惜手段來救她。

Van Helsing 凡・赫辛

　　我是個住在阿姆斯特丹的教授，也是一位醫生。我專治奇特的病症。我以前的一個學生約翰・史華德醫生，要我去倫敦幫忙醫治一個生病的年輕女孩。我想知道她到底發生什麼事了。

[第一章] 外西凡尼亞之旅

p. 14-15 1897 年年初，倫敦的律師強納生·哈克，從倫敦到外西凡尼亞去見一位名叫德古拉伯爵的客戶。哈克從事房地產業，而那位伯爵想在倫敦置產。以下是哈克的日記：

五月三號

　　德古拉伯爵叫我待在比斯特里察的金冠飯店，這是位於喀爾巴阡山山腳下一個風景秀麗的小鎮。當我一抵達時，旅館老闆的太太就給了我一封信。

　　信上說：

> 吾友：
>
> 歡迎來到喀爾巴阡，今晚好好地睡一覺吧。明天下午三點會有一部前往布科維納鎮的公共馬車，我已經幫你預訂了一個位子。當你坐到博格關口時，你就會碰到我的車夫，他會帶你來我這兒。
>
> 友　德古拉

五月四號

　　當我詢問旅館老闆有關伯爵的事時，他的舉止很怪異。之前，他可以聽懂我說的簡單德文，但是當我問到德古拉時，他卻告訴我他聽不懂，他和太太兩人面面相覷。最後，在我不斷地追問下，他們才告訴我他們什麼都不知道，然後還做出了畫十字架的手勢。一切都顯得詭異極了。

p. 16–17 正當我打包好這趟旅程的行李時，那個老婦人緊張地走進我房裡。

「年輕人，你真的要去嗎？」她問我。

我回答說我非去不可，因為這是我的工作。她問我，我真的知道自己要去哪裡、要去做什麼嗎？最後她還跪下來哀求我不要去。

「這是在幹嘛啊！」我心想。我扶她站起來，堅決地說，這是我的工作，我一定要去，沒有任何事可以阻止我。她擦了擦眼角的淚珠，接著拿下脖子上的十字架，掛到我的脖子上。

「看在你母親的份上。」她離開我房間前說。

這是我在等公共馬車時寫的。旅館附近許多鎮民對我議論紛紛。我從字典裡查了幾個我聽到的字，如果沒錯的話，這些字是 Ordog，意思是撒旦；還有 vrolok，指某個不是狼就是吸血鬼的東西。這些字眼都是一些古怪的迷信。

現在馬車來了，遲到總比不到好。

p. 18–19 五月五號

我現在在德古拉伯爵的城堡裡了。這趟路程花了好幾個小時時間，而且還是一趟奇怪的路程。

我們很快就把旅館拋在後頭，進入一個偏僻的美麗鄉間。在面前的是一片樹木林立的翠綠斜坡，左右都是陡峭的小山。午後的陽光讓這美麗山脈更顯壯麗。

很快地，太陽就沒入我們身後。天色昏暗中乘客躁動了起來，似乎都在催促車夫走快一點。車夫用長鞭殘忍地抽打馬匹加速，接著兩側山陵就閉合起來。我們進入博格關口了。

顯然大家正在期待什麼刺激的事情發生，然而儘管我問了每個乘客，卻沒人願意給我一點解釋。我在找帶我去伯爵住處的車夫。我以為在暗中會看到燈光，但卻漆黑一片。

我正想著我該怎麼辦之際，那車夫看著手錶對我說：「這裡沒有馬車在等你，大概是伯爵最後決定不讓你去了。你應該跟著我們去布科維納，然後明天或再隔天就回去，大後天回去更好啦。」

p. 20-21 但是就在他說出這些話沒多久，另一輛馬車就從我們後面追了過來，讓我們的馬匹躁動了起來，同行乘客全都驚叫，做出畫十字架的手勢。

四匹俊美的馬拉著新馬車，並排在我們旁邊。那個車夫是一個高個子的男人，有著棕色的長山羊鬍，一頂大黑帽遮掩了臉龐，掩人耳目，但在我們油燈光下他的眼睛似乎在發紅。

他對車夫說：「朋友，你今晚早到了。」

車夫結結巴巴地回答說：「那個英國先生趕時間。」

對此，陌生人說：「我想那是因為你希望他繼續前往布科維納。朋友，你騙不過我的。我知道的事可多了，而且我的馬飛奔得很快。」

他說著露出微笑，燈光下露出他冷酷無情的嘴，鮮紅的嘴唇，和一口雪象牙白的銳利牙齒。

「把那位先生的行李給我。」他說。我的行李很快被遞送到另一輛馬車上。

在換馬車時，新車夫跳下車幫我就坐，他緊握住我的手臂，然後跳回座位，抖動韁繩，接著我們便搖搖晃晃地飛馳在夜裡。

p. 22-23 就是在這裡，我整個旅程甚至變得更加詭異。一開始，我以為我們在繞圈圈。我把目光聚焦在天際的山頂，突然領悟到我們其實沿著那個關口在繞一個大圈圈。這時，我們已經接近關口的背面了。

我不記得自己有睡著，但是我的確睡著了。我們彷彿走了漫漫長路，馬車突然停下來。我下意識地醒來，看到我們身處一個古老傾頹的城堡庭院中，就在一扇大木門前。

那車夫已拿著我的行李站在地上，和先前一樣用力地抓住我，扶我下馬車。然後他不發一語又跳上馬車，甩動韁繩，馬車一轉彎就消失了蹤影。

我一個人站在那裡不知所措，腦中浮現許多疑問。我來到了什麼樣的地方？我踏入了怎樣的一個恐怖旅程？

這些疑問被巨大的開門聲打斷。一個老人站在那兒，除了長長的小鬍子，臉修得很乾淨，一身黑衣，手拿一盞油燈。

他全身上下甚至連蒼白的臉上都找不到一絲顏色。他用右手非常正式地向我示意。他的英文非常好，但說話的聲調很古怪。

p. 24~25 「歡迎來我家，請進，不要拘束。」

我踏進門檻的那一刻，他用手抓住了我的手。他的手感覺不到任何生氣，但卻擁有和車夫一樣神奇的力量。我驚訝了好一會兒，還以為他就是車夫。為了確認起見，我突然喊了聲：「德古拉伯爵？」

他非常正式地對我欠身回應道：「我就是德古拉，我要向你表達歡迎之意，哈克先生。請進，你來吃點東西，休息一下。」

他拎著我的行李沿著走廊走，告訴我現在已經很晚了，所以僕人們都休息了。我們走上一道蜿蜒的樓梯，穿過一條長廊，到盡頭處他打開一扇厚重的門。
我很高興在門後面看到一間明亮的餐廳，在大大的壁爐裡，明亮熾熱的爐火正熊熊燃燒著。

伯爵打開了另一扇門，通向一間用柴火燒暖的大臥房。伯爵把我的行李放在裡面說：「等你整理好，就會看到餐廳已經備好你的晚餐了。」

p. 26–27 我所有的疑慮和害怕都消失了。我發現自己餓壞了，在迅速梳洗後就去吃東西。主人優雅地對我揮揮手，指向餐桌，說道：「請享用晚餐，很抱歉，我已經先用過餐了。」

晚餐後，我們一起坐在爐火邊。我仔細端詳他，因為他有很多奇異的特徵。他的臉部線條修長嶙峋，鼻子高高瘦瘦的，額頭高而飽滿，豐厚的白髮貼著頭皮往後梳。伯爵的眉毛很粗，兩邊眉毛幾乎連成一線。

他的嘴巴看起來殘酷無情，就算是微笑時也一樣。我可以看到他兩顆尖銳得驚人的白牙，從異常紅潤的嘴唇中突了出來。相較於嘴唇，他臉上其他的部分更顯蒼白。

他的手指短而寬，還長著長長的尖指甲。當他傾身貼近我時，我可從他呼吸中聞到一股腐爛味，令我作嘔，而伯爵見到我的反應便收身回去。

「你一定累了，」他說：「你的臥房已經準備好了。明天你可以睡到自然醒，我會外出，下午才會回來。所以好好地睡吧。祝你有個好夢。」

p. 28–29 **五月七號**

隔天，我很晚才吃早餐，之後我在圖書室碰到了伯爵。那裡有很多英文書籍，我問他我是不是隨時都可以來圖書室。

他回答：「當然。」又說：「除了上鎖的房間，城堡的任何地方都可以去。這裡是在外西凡尼亞，不是英國，我們的習慣和你們不同，你可能會感覺這裡很多事都很奇怪。」

說到這裡話匣子打開了，最後話題轉到了生意上。

「來吧，告訴我倫敦還有你幫我準備的房子。」他說。

我拿出了一份一個名為卡費斯大莊園的文件。伯爵事先已經描述過他所想要的條件，而卡費斯莊園剛好完全符合。這是座在中古世紀建造的古宅，從當時就不斷擴建至今。它有部分看起來像座小城堡，有著厚厚的城牆和厚重的大門。我請他在必要的文件上簽名，再將文件放進一個信封裡，另隨附一封寫給老闆的信。

當我處理完時，他說：「真高興莊園又大又舊，我們家族很古老，住新房子會要了我的命。老房子有很多陰暗隱密的地方，我就愛這些幽暗處。」

我們又多聊了一些話，大都聊到英國。突然間伯爵跳起來說：「哎呀，天都亮了，我真不像話，讓你都不能睡了。你可別再說話這麼有趣了，不然我會忘了時間的。」

他彬彬有禮地鞠躬後迅即離去。

p.30–31 弗拉德化身為德古拉伯爵

伯蘭．史杜克讓德古拉聞名於世，但弗拉德．采佩什就沒那麼有名了。采佩什這位 15 世紀的王子，是史杜克創作邪惡德古拉伯爵的靈感來源。

采佩什是瓦拉幾亞王子，這是羅馬尼亞位於外西凡尼亞附近的領土。采佩什的生活並不快樂，因他被（鄂圖曼帝國）土耳其人綁架充當人質數年。他在伊斯坦堡聽聞父兄全被鄰近地區的一個貴族殺害的消息，17 歲時便帶領一支土耳其軍隊，為自己重新取回瓦拉幾亞王位。

在成功奪權後，他對殺害父兄的貴族採取了恐怖的報復行動。他用尖棍刺穿年老的貴族，並強迫年輕貴族和家人到另個城鎮建築城堡。築堡工程極其艱鉅，造成死傷無數，但眾人最終還是建造完成德古拉城堡。

在統治期間，弗拉德用棍棒刺穿的方式殺害了數千名敵人，而這也是他「穿刺公」綽號的由來，也或許是史杜克想到要殺害德古拉的唯一方式，就是用木樁刺穿他心臟的靈感由來吧。

[第二章] 德古拉城堡的囚犯

`p. 32–33` **五月八號**

我開始覺得這地方有些怪怪的。我在日記裡只寫實際發生的事，以壓抑自己的想像力。

睡了幾小時起來後，我開始刮鬍子，刮鬍照的鏡子就掛在窗戶旁。突然間，我覺得有隻手在我的肩膀上。我聽到伯爵對我說：「早安。」

我大吃一驚，因為我並沒有在鏡中看到他。我驚訝得跳了起來，輕輕地割傷了自己。鏡中仍然不見伯爵的身影，即使他就在我的右肩上方！

接著我看到了下巴的傷口和血。我一轉頭，伯爵看到我的臉時眼神燃燒著狂怒。他突然抓住我的喉嚨，我往後退，他的手碰到掛著十字架念珠的鍊子，讓他瞬間安靜了下來，那股狂怒瞬間消逝，讓我不敢相信他剛剛曾那麼生氣過。

「小心，你怎麼割傷自己了。」他說：「在這裡，割傷自己可是會比你想像的還危險喔。」他沒拿走鏡子，又丟下一句：「這東西只會帶來麻煩，扔了吧！」

p. 34 他用可怕的雙手使勁地打開窗戶，把鏡子丟出去。鏡子在下面庭院的石頭上裂成了無數碎片，然後他便不發一語就走了。

我走進餐廳，早餐已經準備好，但四處都找不到伯爵，所以就獨自一人吃早餐。奇怪的是，到目前為止，我都還沒看過伯爵吃喝東西，他一定是個很怪的人。

早餐後，我在城堡裡做了點小小的探險。這裡有門，那裡也有門，到處都是門，而且都鎖住了！除了窗戶，根本沒有門可以打開。我變成囚犯了。

在我明白這點後，聽到下面有門關上。我小心地返回我房間，看到伯爵正在整理床鋪，這證實了我的懷疑：這房子裡根本沒有僕人，現在我確定駕馬車的一定就是伯爵本人。

為什麼比斯特里察的居民都特別為我感到擔憂？感謝那個把十字架掛在我脖子上的善良婦人！它帶給我一絲慰藉。

p. 36-37 五月十二號

昨晚，伯爵向我詢問運輸的法律問題。

他說：「假設，我想要寄貨物，例如寄到紐卡索、杜倫或是多佛。貨物抵達時雇用律師去幫我領取，是不是會比較輕鬆一點？」

我盡量向他解釋一切，他滿意後，突然站起來問我：「除了寫給霍金斯先生的第一封信外，你還有寫其他信嗎？」

我回答說沒有。

「那現在寫吧，我的年輕朋友，寫給霍金斯先生和其他人，告訴他們，從現在開始你要待在這裡一個月。」他說。

「你要我待那麼久嗎？」這個念頭讓我的心都涼了。

「我不接受拒絕。你的老闆派你來為我服務的，不是嗎？」

除了接受，我還能怎麼辦？這事關霍金斯先生的利益，我得為他著想，不能只想到我自己。

除此，德古拉伯爵說話時，眼裡和舉止傳達出了一些訊息，讓我想起自己是個囚犯。就算我想離開，我也沒有選擇。於是我帶著俱增的恐懼，寫了幾封信。

p. 38–39　他離開後，我回到自己的房裡。一會兒，我望向窗外。看到沐浴在黃色月光下遼闊美麗的鄉間景緻，我找到了一絲自由的氣息與安詳。

當我從窗戶探身出去時，發現下方有東西在動。伯爵的頭從下方的窗戶探出來。一開始我還覺得這巧合很有趣，但當我看到他整個人緩緩地從窗戶裡現身，像隻黑色的大昆蟲開始爬下城牆時，我一陣作噁，心生恐懼。他的臉朝下，黑色斗篷展開像雙翅膀一樣。

起初，我不敢相信自己的眼睛，心想是月光讓我眼花了，但是我一直看著，我確定那不是錯覺。

這是個什麼樣的人，還是說是什麼怪物呢？我覺得這個令人毛骨悚然的地方，已經恐怖得讓我待不下去了。我很害怕，害怕極了，卻無處可逃。

p. 40–41　**五月十五號**

我又看到伯爵穿著昆蟲裝離開城堡了。他離開後，我決定要深入探索城堡。我試過所有門都上了鎖，最後終於在樓梯最上方找到一個門沒上鎖，只是卡得很緊。我用盡吃奶的力氣，把門推開一個可以進去的空隙。

我發現自己身處在一個可能是古早前，城堡女士用的房間裡。我喜歡這房間和景觀，所以我坐下來寫日記。

後記：五月十六號早上

我發誓我沒有瘋，但是這裡真的有某東西在試煉我的神智。我認為這裡有比伯爵更恐怖的邪惡野獸，但也不得不信，只要我還有利用價值，伯爵就會保我平安，這想法會令人發狂。

伯爵曾警告我不要在別的房間睡著時，我被嚇到了。只是在我寫完日記時突然覺得很睏，當時我還在樓梯最上方的房間裡。月光是那麼柔和，房內沙發引人躺下。於是，我在沙發上伸伸懶腰便睡著了。

p. 42–43 我突然醒來，或是說以為醒了。我是在做夢吧，因為房裡還有三位女郎和我一起。這彷彿是夢，因月光下的女郎竟無影子。

其中兩人是黑髮女郎，有著深色大眼睛，眼神十分銳利，像是透出紅光一樣；另位女郎滿頭金髮，眼睛像淡色的藍寶石。三人都有著閃亮的白牙，在豐潤紅唇襯托下，白牙有如珍珠般閃耀。

我感覺到了渴望，同時又極度恐懼。她們竊竊私語著，然後三個人都笑了。她們銀鈴般悅耳的笑聲，透著毫無人性的殘酷。金髮女郎羞怯地搖搖頭，另兩個則在一旁慫恿著。

一人說：「去吧，妳先上，等一下換我們。妳有權先開始。」

另一個則附和說：「他既年輕又強壯，夠我們三個親吻了。」

我靜靜地躺著，帶著既苦惱又愉悅的期待，從我睫毛下瞄出去。金髮女郎走向前，在我上方彎下腰來。我可以聞到她的氣息，那是一種苦甜參半的味道，有蜜糖的甜味，但又帶點血腥味。她既令人感到興奮又讓人嫌惡。

當她拱起脖子時，竟然像動物般舔著自己的唇。她的頭

146

愈彎愈低，嘴唇移到我的下巴下，彷若就要咬住我的喉嚨一樣。我可以感覺到她呼在我脖子上的熱氣，我心噗通噗通狂跳，閉上眼睛等待著。

p. 44–45 啊，但突然間，我感覺到伯爵就像一陣暴風突然現身這房裡。我看到他強壯的手，抓住金髮女郎纖細的脖子，用巨大的力量將脖子往後拉，她藍色的眼睛憤怒地變形了。

　　而那伯爵！他的狂怒令人無法想像！他的眼睛如地獄火燄般火紅地燃燒。他把那個女郎丟出去，舉起手指著其他兩個，用一種劃破空氣的聲音說：「明明我下令禁止，妳們居然還敢碰他？他是我的人！」

　　接著，伯爵溫柔低語說：「我答應妳們，在我處理完我的年輕朋友後，妳們就可以隨意親吻他了，但是現在，給我滾吧！」

　　我半瞇著眼睛看著，她們似乎消逝在月光中，從窗戶飛散出去了。接著，恐懼壓倒了我，我筋疲力盡地失去了意識。

p. 46–47 ## 五月十九號

　　我的死期逐漸接近中。昨晚伯爵以極客氣的方式要我寫下三封信。第一封說我在這裡的工作已接近尾聲，我在幾天內就可以啟程回家；另一封說我在寫完信的隔天早上會出發。第三封則說我已經離開城堡抵達比斯特里察了。

　　我只能照辦，因為我身陷在伯爵的地盤上。

　　因此，我裝作沒事的樣子，並問他我該在信上押上什麼日期。他說第一封是 6 月 12 號，第二封是 6 月 19 日，而第三封則是 6 月 29 日。

　　現在我知道自己可以活多久了，上帝保佑我！

五月二十八號

　　有個可以逃跑的機會，或至少可以捎個信回家。一群吉普賽人來到了城堡，也許他們會幫我。

　　我試圖和他們搭上線，但都失敗了。一開始，我從窗戶喊他們時，他們對我似乎還滿客氣的，但沒多久，他們就對我視而不見了。

p. 48–49 六月十七號

　　今天早上我坐在床邊時，聽到鞭子揮動的霹啪聲，還有馬匹踏上石階的沉重腳步聲。

　　我很高興急忙跑到窗邊，看到兩輛很大的馬車，每輛都由八匹健壯的馬拉著，由斯洛伐克人駕駛。車夫們戴著寬帽，繫著飾滿釘子的大皮帶，披著髒羊皮，穿著高統靴。

　　我對他們叫喊著，他們傻乎乎地抬頭看我。那群吉普賽人的頭子不知道說了什麼，他們都笑了。

　　之後，不管我再怎麼費力，他們都不再看我一眼。他們的馬車載著大大的方形箱子，上頭還有粗繩做成的把手。從斯洛伐克人搬箱子的樣子來看，這些箱子很明顯是空的。箱子都被卸下後，他們就乘車離開了。

六月二十五號

　　我得在白天採取一些行動。我還沒有在日光下看過伯爵出現，會不會是人家醒著時他卻都在睡覺？

　　要是我能進去他的房間就好了！要是敢的話，倒有個方法。我曾見過他從窗戶爬出來，為何我不能模仿他，從他的窗戶爬進去呢？這是個可怕的冒險，但我得試試。

p. 50-51 **同一天稍晚**

我成功了。我進到伯爵房間，房裡空蕩蕩，只有角落有一堆黃金，還有各國和好幾個年代的錢幣。厚重的大房門敞開著。我在又破又舊的城堡裡到處搜尋，終於在地下室有了發現。

在一個地下房間，我看到了 50 個左右的大箱子，箱裡裝滿一半剛掘出的泥土。箱子大都沒有蓋上蓋子，而其中一個箱子裡就躺著伯爵！

我的血頓時冷卻，伯爵看起來像是死掉或睡著了。嘴唇一樣很鮮紅，卻完全沒有動靜，沒有脈搏、呼吸和心跳的跡象。

我想他身上應該有鑰匙。但是當我去找鑰匙時，我看到他像死人般的眼睛，充滿仇恨，於是我拔腿就跑。

我從窗戶離開伯爵的房間，爬牆回到自己的房間。我氣喘吁吁地倒在床上，想理出個頭緒。

p. 52-53 **六月二十九號**

今天我在圖書室裡睡著了，後來被伯爵給叫醒，他正陰森森地看著我。

他說：「朋友，明天我們就要離別了。你回到你美麗的英國，我也要回去工作。等我的員工和我走後，我的馬車就會來送你去博格關口，在那裡就可以接上從布科維納到比斯特里察的馬車了。」

我不相信他的話，所以我問：「我為什麼不能在今天晚上走？」

他露出微笑，那種柔善的魔鬼笑容，顯示他心懷鬼胎。他走到窗戶旁說：「等等，你仔細聽。」

外面傳來很多狼的嚎叫聲，好像是他一舉手，那聲音就出現了。我知道有那種野獸在樹林遊蕩，夜裡就逃不了了。

一兩分鐘後我回到自己的房間。我最後一次看到德古拉伯爵，就是他對著我親吻自己的手，眼神裡還帶著勝利的紅色光芒。

p.54-55 六月三十號

這可能是我在這本日記寫下最後的話了。今天我又爬下城牆。我走到伯爵躺著的箱子旁，這回箱子蓋上了，但沒有釘上釘子。我需要前門的鑰匙，所以把蓋子搬移一旁，這時我嚇了一跳。

伯爵躺在箱裡，貌似年輕了一半的歲數，嘴巴紅甚從前，唇上有著鮮血，從嘴角流下，一直流到下巴與脖子。他看起來就像一隻肥水蛭，剛吸飽血正在休息一樣。

我彎下身碰觸他時全身顫抖著，身上每根神經都感到噁心不已，但我還得繼續搜尋。我到處都摸遍了，就是找不到鑰匙。我站在那裡思索，聽到吉普賽人快活的聲音從隧道中傳了下來。

我迅速跑掉，爬回自己房裡，不久就聽到吉普賽人車隊離開的聲音。現在，城堡裡只剩我獨自一人和那三個恐怖的女人了。我應該再試著從城牆爬下庭院，我得在這恐怖之地找出條路來。

如果這真的是我最後的留筆，那麼再見了。米娜，我愛妳。

[第三章] 死亡之船

p. 58-59 當強納生在外西凡尼亞時,他的未婚妻米娜正在寫信給好友露西,露西最近要和一名英國紳士訂婚了。

米娜為露西感到開心,但她也有點擔心強納生。強納生出差好一段時間了,而且信都寫得很短。

為了慶祝露西的訂婚,並舒緩一下米娜對強納生的憂心,兩個年輕女孩決定一起到一個叫做惠特比的海濱小鎮度假,她們租了一個賓館房間,可以俯瞰海洋、小教堂和相鄰的墓園。

米娜和露西習慣坐在墓園墓碑上,因為從墓碑看到的景致很美麗。一天,米娜獨自一人坐著,一名士兵從旁經過。他停下來和米娜說話,卻又不斷地望著海上遠處一艘奇怪的船。

「那艘船航行得很怪,從外表看來,這是一艘俄國船,但是它卻以最詭異的方式四處漂移。每陣風吹來,它就隨著改變方向,好像沒人駕駛一樣。相信我們明天這時就會聽到關於這艘船的事。」士兵說。

p. 60-61 那名士兵的預測是對的。隔天,就在一場強烈的暴風雨後,米娜在惠特比的地方報上看到了下面的報導:

八月八號

有史以來最大最突然的一場暴風雨剛侵襲了本地，並造成了詭異的奇特現象。接近十點時，濕熱空氣變得非常悶。午夜後不久，一道奇怪的聲音從海上傳來。暴風雨毫無預警地迅速來襲，極為不尋常。

海浪不斷地猛烈上升，將平靜無浪的海水，變成一頭咆哮、貪婪的怪獸。強風像雷聲般的呼嘯著，風勢大到連強壯的成年男子都很難站得住。

一陣又冷又濕的海霧到來，圍觀的人群認為那是溺斃水手的鬼魂。偶爾當霧氣稍散，在閃電的亮光下暴露出的海浪，高得像座小山。

隱約可見一些企圖衝進港口的小漁船。東峭壁上最近才裝設完成的探照燈被打開，每當一艘船安全地抵達，旁觀群眾就會發出大大的歡呼聲。

突然，探照燈發現了一個讓大家膽戰心驚的景象。在暴風雨前就被照到的那艘外國貨輪，現在位置更近了，有可能會觸礁擱淺，情況危急。

p. 62–63

接著又來了一陣海霧，規模史上最大。這團海霧讓大家都看不到即將發生的災難。探照燈的光線，就固定在可能會出現撞擊聲的礁石方向。

風向突然轉移到東北方，海霧被吹開。在碼頭間，可見船在浪頭猛烈地跳躍，那艘奇怪的船的船帆尚未被風吹滿前，就不停地搖晃著。

探照燈密切照著它，船安全抵達港口了。燈光照出一個讓眾人嚇得打哆嗦的景象。綁在舵輪上的是一具頭垂下的屍體，頭隨著船身搖晃恐怖地來回晃動著，而甲板上看不到任何活人或死人。當大家發現這艘船是在這個死人的手中安全進港口時，每人都湧起了敬畏心。但是那艘船卻無法減速下來，它衝過了碼頭，以嚇人的撞擊聲撞上惠特比小教堂下面的沙灘。

在隔天的報紙上，又出現了以下的報導：

> 　　海巡員已確定那艘在暴風雨中擱淺的神秘船隻就是狄米特號，是從瓦爾納出航的俄國船。綁在舵輪上的屍體就是船長，他的航海日誌被發現在一旁。

p. 64–65 吸血鬼的傳說

　　伯蘭・史杜克創造了舉世最有名的吸血鬼，但他並非第一個想到吸血鬼的人。有關吸血鬼的傳說，早在許多文化中流傳千年。

　　印度民間傳說中有一種叫做「羅剎」的怪物，牠的行為舉止就像吸血鬼一樣。牠以人形模樣出現，卻又帶著些許動物的特徵，像是爪子或毒牙。牠們不只會喝受害者的血，還吃他們的肉。要消滅牠們只能用火、陽光或一種能夠摧毀牠們靈魂的宗教儀式。

　　在墨西哥，吸血鬼大多是女性，被稱為 Tlahuelpuchi（吸血巫婆）。她們帶著吸血鬼的詛咒出生，但要到青春期才會知道自己的命運。這些吸血鬼每月都要喝一次嬰兒的血，否則就會死掉。大蒜、洋蔥和金屬皆可用來驅趕吸血鬼。

　　在歐洲的黑暗時代，當有人在睡夢中神秘暴斃時，人們就會開始說一定是被吸血鬼所殺，因此吸血鬼也就代表了死亡。為了防止死亡發生，村民會挖開墳墓尋找吸血鬼。而那些未腐爛的屍體，會被當成是造成村裡死亡事件發生的吸血鬼。為了「殺死」吸血鬼，村民們會砍下死屍的頭，或將心臟挖出來，伯蘭・史杜克創作德古拉伯爵吸血鬼的作品，便是受到這些歐洲傳說的影響。

[第四章] 黑暗的威脅

p. 66–67 米娜·莫瑞的日記

八月十號

　　今天那個可憐船長的喪禮非常地感人。這裡每個人都將船長視為英雄，雖然他最後看起來有點失去理智，但是他甚至在自己死後還把船帶回了港口。

　　可憐的露西心神不寧。她一直沒有好好地休息，我想她應該是做惡夢了，但她是不會説的。她從小就會夢遊，現在又開始了。

八月十二號

　　昨晚我醒來時，發現露西已不在我們房裡了。我去我們常去的教堂，看到一個穿著白色衣服的身影躺在一塊墓碑上。我走近看到一個黑色身影俯身傾向她。我大叫著往前跑，那身影轉頭看著我。我看到了帶著憎恨的紅色眼睛和蒼白臉龐。

　　然後那身影便消失無影。我發現露西睡在墓碑上，我把一件斗篷繫在她肩上。在繫斗篷時，我看到她脖子上有血滴，我一定是用別針刺到她了。

p. 68–69 **八月十四號**

　　露西的情況愈來愈不好。她會在半夜醒來想走出房間，到白天就非常蒼白虛弱。

　　我終於收到強納生的信了。他生病了，現在正在布達佩斯的一家醫院裡。我得去找他，但我又不敢留下露西一個人。

於是我寫信給露西的未婚夫亞瑟。亞瑟很快就會來，他答應要帶露西和她母親回到他在倫敦的住所。只要他一到，我就要前往布達佩斯。希望我不在時露西能夠康復！

八月二十四號

在經過漫長旅程後，我終於抵達強納生所在的布達佩斯醫院。他既虛弱又疲累，但至少他還活著。他受到了一些可怕的驚嚇。醒來時，他跟我要他的外套，他想拿外套裡的東西。我看到了他的日記，他看到我盯著日記，不一會兒，他握著我的手告訴我，他深深地愛著我。

接著，他叫我看看他的日記，但是他不想再跟我談論此事。所以我知道了強納生在德古拉城堡裡所受的折磨。這一切都非常地詭異，但我不會和他討論這些事。他活下來了，而且我們也在一起了。

p. 70–71 ## 九月二號

強納生已經恢復了大半健康與活力。昨天我們在一個布達佩斯的小教堂裡結婚了。我們十分相愛，明天我們就要開始返回英國的漫長旅程了。

米娜和強納生回到了英國，開始他們的新生活。但是當他們抵達時，米娜發現了一封正等著她的信，那是亞瑟‧霍伍德寫的。信裡有個不幸的消息：露西死了！

亞瑟・霍伍德的日記

　　露西和她的母親前來倫敦和我住在一起。一開始，她看起來很開心，也沒有顯露出在惠特比所受折磨的疲累或虛弱的跡象。但一個星期後，卻突然病倒臥床。

　　我請來好友傑克・史華德醫師，他隨即趕到。他在露西的脖子上發現了兩個小小的奇怪傷口，並判定她流失了大量的血液。但是怎麼會這樣？她的床上一滴血都沒有啊！

　　在困惑不解的情況下，史華德醫生求教了他的老教授亞伯拉罕・凡・赫辛醫師。這位學識淵博的先生非常地好心，他一聽說露西的詳情後就立刻趕來了。

　　p. 72-73 凡・赫辛醫生到達後，我們都來到露西的房間。她就像死人般地蒼白，嘴唇齒齦不見血色，臉上顴骨也明顯突出，呼吸微弱得聽不太出來。露西一動也不動地躺著，好像沒有力氣說話，所以有好一會兒我們都沉默不語。後來凡・赫辛醫師向我們示意，我們便輕聲地走出房間。

　　我們一關上門，凡・赫辛醫師就喊著：「天啊！這太可怕了，我們沒有時間浪費了，她會因為缺血死掉，要馬上輸血才行。亞瑟，你是我們三個當中最年輕也最強壯的一個。」

　　他沒有再多說什麼。我發誓我會把血給露西，若有需要，最後一滴血都給她也再所不惜。凡・赫辛醫生立刻進行了輸血。很明顯地，他的方法是對的。有了我的血液注入露西的血管，病情有了顯著的改善。

　　隔天，我得前往父親倫敦郊外的住處。他病重，我得去看他。我情非得已只好將露西留給史華德醫師和凡・赫辛醫師照顧，他們看起來應該有辦法讓露西恢復健康。

p. 74–75 **史華德醫師的日記**

在亞瑟前去探視生病的父親後沒多久，凡‧赫辛醫生告訴我，他要回他阿姆斯特丹的家一趟，去拿一些和露西的病情相關的書。

他告訴我：「我只離開幾天，你要看好露西，特別是晚上。放張椅子在她床邊，別讓她起來夢遊，這點很重要。如果你非睡不可，就白天時再睡。」

對這個奇怪的請求他並未多做解釋，只說他需要參考一些放在家裡的書。

我告訴露西母親，凡‧赫辛醫師指示我得熬夜陪露西，她聽了很不屑，還指出她女兒的精神體力都在恢復當中。但我很堅持，並且開始準備長期的守夜工作。

露西並沒有表示反對，反而用充滿感激的眼神看著我。一段時間後，她好像已經累得快睡著了，但她又振作起精神，把睡蟲趕走，顯見她並不想睡，所以我立刻挑起話題。

「妳不想睡嗎？」

「不想，我很害怕。」

「親愛的小姐，妳今晚可以安心地睡。我在這裡看著妳，我保證不會有任何事情發生的。」

「你對我太好了，那我睡了！」她話一說完，就寬心地鬆了一口氣，躺回床上睡著了。

p. 76–77 我整晚看著她。她自始至終都睡得很沉、很安穩，連個翻身都沒有。她的臉上浮現了微笑，顯然沒有夢魘來干擾她內心的平靜。

我看顧露西已經兩夜了。白天我還是在精神病院盡職工作，但這樣的工作時呈已經開始挑戰我的體力了。第三天晚上，我來到露西住所時，我看到她已經起身，而且精神很好。

她跟我握手，仔細地看著我的臉，跟我說：「今晚你不要再熬夜了，你已累壞了，我已經恢復健康了。事實上，我好得很。要是要熬夜，也該是我陪著你一起熬。」

我沒有再反對就去吃晚餐了。接著露西帶我到樓上，給我看她臥房旁的一間房，溫暖的爐火正燃燒著。

「現在，你得待在這裡。我會開著這扇門和我的門，你可以躺在沙發上。我要有什麼需要，我會叫你，你就可以馬上過來我這裡了。」她說。

我只好答應，因為我已累壞沒法再熬夜了。所以我再度要她承諾有事一定要叫我後，就躺在沙發上，把萬事都拋諸腦後了。

p. 78-79 我意識到教授的手放在我的頭上，不一會兒我就醒過來了。

「我們的病人怎麼樣了？」他說。

「我們去看看吧！」我回答。

我們進到露西的房間時，看到了一幅可怕的景象。可憐的露西躺在床上，比以往還要蒼白許多。她的唇是蠟白的，齒齦從牙齒整個縮起來，就像有時我們會在久病過世的屍體上所看到的一樣。

凡・赫辛立刻用手摸了她的心跳。

「還來得及，還在跳，只是很虛弱。我們之前所做的都白費了，得從頭來過。現在這裡沒有年輕亞瑟的血可用了，親愛的約翰，這次要拜託你親自上陣了。」他說。

他又輸了一次血，這回是用我的血。露西安穩地睡到白天。她醒來時，雖然不像先前狀況那麼好，但也是精神奕奕，一副健康的模樣。

那天晚上，凡·赫辛給了露西一串看起來像花朵的項鍊。起初她很開心，但後來說：「喔，教授，我想您一定在開我玩笑吧，咦，這花只不過是普普通通的大蒜啊。」

「可不只喔，親愛的！」凡·赫辛醫師斷然地回答：「我從不開玩笑的，我做的事都是有目的的。現在在這裡坐一會，別亂動。約翰，我的朋友，你來幫我用大蒜裝飾整個房間。」

p. 80–81 教授的舉動很奇怪，我在任何書上都未曾聽聞。一開始，他先把窗戶關緊，牢牢閂緊。接下來，他拿了一把花，塗遍所有窗框，又用蒜頭來擦門把，門的上上下下和內外也都抹上了蒜頭，壁爐的四周也是。

當露西在床上躺好時，他就把一圈的大蒜固定在她脖子四周，丟下最後一句話給她：「小心千萬別弄亂了。就算空氣悶熱不通，也不要打開窗戶或門。」

「好，我不會的。還有萬分感激兩位。喔，我何德何能，能讓兩位朋友這樣地保護我。」露西說。

我們離開後，凡·赫辛說：「我趕了兩天的路，白天時還看了好些書，今晚總算可以安穩地睡覺了。明天早上來接我，我們一起來看看我們美麗的小姐。」

隔天早上，我們很早就到了，還碰到了露西的母親。她告訴我們，她已經進去過露西的房間。她發現空氣都是濃濃的大蒜味，她很擔心，所以把窗戶都打開，還把露西脖子上的大蒜項鍊拿起來。

她說話時，凡·赫辛的臉色一陣灰白，他什麼都沒跟她說，但她一離開後，他重重地跌坐在椅子上。

p. 82–83 「天啊！天啊！」他說：「這個可憐的母親做了什麼？就因為她的疏忽，就因為想給女兒新鮮的空氣，結果她失去了寶貝女兒的鮮血和靈魂。」

但突然，他從絕望中忽然跳了起來。

「快，我們得採取行動！現在換我捐血幫露西輸血了。」他說。

我們又再一次輸血，也再次看到健康流回露西蒼白的臉頰。

輸血後，我們讓露西安穩地睡在床上。我必須回精神病院補上我所落後的工作進度。那天下午，我沒有接到凡・赫辛的傳喚，所以我帶著疲憊的身軀，回家好好地休息了一晚。

早上時，我被嚇了一大跳。突然有封電報，是凡・赫辛在前一天寫的。上面寫著：

> 我得去辦事，今晚無法看顧露西。很重要！

天啊！我昨晚應該待在她那裡的！驚恐中，我立刻前往亞瑟的住所。我一到就碰到剛進門的凡・赫辛。

「怎麼？你沒在這裡過夜嗎？你沒收到我的電報嗎？」他說。

我們按前門的門鈴，但沒有回應。我們急忙跑到屋後，從廚房窗戶望進去。四個僕人像死人一樣躺在地上。凡・赫辛打破窗戶，我們衝了進去，從他們吃力的呼吸和已開瓶的酒味，我們旋即明白他們被下藥了。

p. 84–85 我們跑到露西的房間，甩開大門。我該怎麼形容我們所看到的？床上躺著的是露西和她的母親。母親臉上倉白，滿臉驚恐，她一定是死於心臟病發。露西就躺在她身旁，她皮膚白得跟粉筆一樣，喉嚨露出來，有兩個小小的傷口，看起來毫無血色，傷得很嚴重。

　　教授一句話都沒說，俯身彎向露西，傾聽她生命的跡象。突然間，他跳起來對我大叫說：「還有救，快把僕人們都叫醒。」

　　凡・赫辛叫他們為露西準備了熱水澡，然後叫我去找亞瑟來。

　　當天下午，亞瑟心情消沈地回來。他父親剛剛過世，而現在未婚妻又陷入死亡邊緣。他走進她房裡，跪在床邊。她勉強地維持著清醒。她看到亞瑟時，說：「親愛的，再靠近一點，好讓我親吻你。」

　　亞瑟開始靠過去，但是凡・赫辛抓住他，把他往後拉。露西突然憤怒地發出嘶嘶聲，她的牙齒又白又長，但臉又倏然柔和了下來，手握亞瑟的手。

　　「親愛的，我愛你。」然後她就死了。

　　「可憐的女孩，一切都結束了。」我說。

　　「不，才正要開始而已。」凡・赫辛小聲地說。

[第五章] 美麗的女士

p. 88–89 **史華德醫師的故事接續**

　　在露西和她母親的喪禮後，報紙上有奇怪的新聞報導了附近小孩所發生的事。幾個小孩消失整晚，回家後一直在討論：「一個美麗的女士」。警方把這些話當成是小孩在模仿大人的話，因而未予以理會。

　　一天下午，凡・赫辛來到我辦公室，把昨天晚上的《西敏公報》塞到我手上。

「你怎麼看這件事？」他往後一站，雙手交叉著問。

那篇報導是有關在漢普斯特被誘騙的孩童。我看到其中一段描述他們的喉嚨上有小小的穿刺傷。我心頭突然冒出一個想法，我說：「不管傷害露西的是什麼，那東西現在正在傷害他們。」

「我擔心事情比這個還嚴重，」凡·赫辛說：「傷口是露西造成的！」

我生氣地站起來說：「凡·赫辛醫生，你瘋了嗎？」

他神情哀痛地看著我，說：「但願我是瘋了。」然後他舉起一把鑰匙，又說：「這是露西墓園的鑰匙，跟我來，我讓你看看。」

p. 90~91 那天晚上，我們進到露西長眠的墓地。但是當凡·赫辛移開她棺木上的石板時，露西的屍體卻不在那裡！

我們在墳墓外等著。不久我們就看到一個穿著白色衣服的身影走進去。我們跟著那個人影進到墳墓裡。凡·赫辛再次移開那塊石板，露西就躺在那裡。她的臉色很白，卻有著血紅色的唇！事實上，她下巴上還有一些血滴！凡·赫辛將她的唇拉下，我看到了染了鮮血的白色長牙。

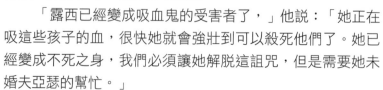

我們迅速離開墓園。凡·赫辛解釋發生什麼事時，我非常地震驚。

「露西已經變成吸血鬼的受害者了，」他說：「她正在吸這些孩子的血，很快她就會強壯到可以殺死他們了。她已經變成不死之身，我們必須讓她解脫這詛咒，但是需要她未婚夫亞瑟的幫忙。」

隔天，我們和亞瑟碰面了。起初，他的反應跟我很像，說凡·赫辛是個胡說八道的瘋子。基於和亞瑟長年的友誼，我讓他鎮定了下來。然後我和凡·赫辛一起說服他當晚去露西的墓園一探。

p. 92–93 和之前一樣，當我們打開露西的墓穴時，她的屍體不見了。我們到外面等著。不久我們看到露西來了，她帶來一個孩子。她看到我們，發出像狂貓般的嘶嘶聲，還把那孩子丟在地上。她冷不防地走向亞瑟，用一種狀似充滿愛意的柔和聲音說話，但其實骨子裡卻冷酷無情。

「來吧，我的丈夫，」她說：「離開他們，來這裡和我一起長眠。」

亞瑟好像被催眠一樣地向她走去，我抓住他的手臂，把他往後拉。凡‧赫辛立刻跳上前，揮舞他的十字架。露西縮了回去，她走到墳墓的入口，還穿過了關閉的門！

我們跟著她走進去，看到她躺在自己的墳墓裡，好像睡著了一樣。凡‧赫辛拿了榔頭和木樁給亞瑟。

「你得讓她解脫，」凡‧赫辛說：「等我開始唸禱詞，你就把木樁釘進她的心臟。」

當凡‧赫辛開始禱告時，亞瑟用榔頭將木樁敲打進了露西的胸口。淚珠從他臉上滑下，她的身體掙扎地扭動著，亞瑟再次敲打木樁。露西的軀體馬上就出現了變化，它變得軟綿綿的，面容也變得安詳了。這回真正的露西現身了，而不是那個她變成的恐怖怪物。她終於解脫了。

p. 94–95 可怕的女吸血鬼

在伯蘭‧史杜克的小說裡，露西變成了一個專門捕食小孩的美麗吸血鬼。而在現實生活中，在匈牙利也有一個女貴族和這故事很雷同。她名叫伊莉莎白‧貝瑟利，1560 年出生於一個有權有勢的匈牙利家族，她有著烏黑的長髮，襯托著光滑白皙的肌膚。很不幸的是，伊莉莎白愛上了自己的美貌。

傳說有一天，那時伊莉莎白已經較年長了，有個女僕在幫她梳頭時扯下了一根頭髮。伊莉莎白很用力地打了那女孩的手，手上的戒指把女孩畫出流血。當血液碰到伊莉莎白的皮膚時，產生了一種帶有青春活力的紅潤。

伊莉莎白對於保持年輕非常地感興趣。她想，只要利用血液就可長保美貌，所以她和僕人開始抓捕當地的年輕女孩，虐待她們，殺害她們，並取光有的血。農人們在城堡外發現無血的屍體，有關伊莉莎白是吸血鬼的謠言就傳開了。

最後匈牙利的首相，也是伊莉莎白的表哥來到城堡，他在那裡發現了年輕女孩的死屍，甚至還有一些等著被殺的女孩。

當地的傳言說，她的鬼魂現在仍流連在城堡附近的喀爾巴阡山。

[第六章] 追捕德古拉

p. 96–97 在露西的喪禮後，米娜和凡·赫辛聯絡，因為他好像知道很多有關她朋友過世的詳情。在米娜聽完了那個詭異的故事後，她把強納生的日記給了他。凡·赫辛就是藉此得知德古拉伯爵以及他即將搬到英國的事情。

在吸血鬼露西被殺之後，凡·赫辛找來史華德醫師、亞瑟、強納生和米娜一起開會。

「我們必須毀滅德古拉伯爵，」他說：「他是一個很強大的吸血鬼。他強迫別人喝下他的血後，他們就變成他的奴隸。他的力氣強如二十個人，而且他很聰明，可以改變自己的外型，變成狼、蝙蝠甚至是薄霧來穿過最細小的裂縫。不過他也有一些弱點，他只能在夜間活動，白天時他會跟真的死了一樣地躺在棺木裡。」

接著，凡·赫辛轉向強納生。

「你說他帶著五十個大箱子離開他在外西凡尼亞的城堡？」

強納生點點頭。

p. 98–99「那我們必須找到所有的箱子，把它們都摧毀。」凡‧赫辛説：「這樣他就沒有地方可以休息，他會愈來愈虛弱，甚至死掉。」

我們該找的地方顯見就是卡費斯，也就是強納生幫伯爵買的莊園。凡‧赫辛一行人發現，與其説卡費斯是一棟豪宅，還不如説它是座古堡。在城堡地底還有味道難聞的潮濕地道。在地道裡，吸血鬼獵人們發現了德古拉的箱子。

他們打開每個箱子，凡‧赫辛將聖水噴灑入內，灑水時還一邊唸著禱詞。最後，他把教堂裡用來象徵耶穌身體的聖餅放在每個棺木裡，但是就在他進行到最後一個棺材前，他們聽到有東西靠近的聲音。

「我們晚了一步，」凡‧赫辛説：「德古拉伯爵已經回來了。」

所有人散開來做好攻擊準備，但是他們看到伯爵進來時，全都被嚇到了。伯爵的行動異常地迅速，凡‧赫辛舉起他的十字架，伯爵就往後退，這個舉動給了凡‧赫辛一行人逃出去的機會。

「快，」凡‧赫辛説：「他知道我們在追蹤他，強納生，他可能會攻擊你的住所。米娜有危險了！」

p. 100–101他們全都趕回強納生家裡，跑上米娜位於樓上的房間。房門上鎖了，強納生説這很不尋常。這群人破門而入，一幅恐怖的景象映入眼簾。米娜就穿著白色睡袍，軟綿綿地站在她床邊，身旁站著一個瘦瘦高高的男人，穿著一身黑衣。他的臉並沒有面向這群人，但他們一看到他的瞬間便認出那就是伯爵。

他的左手緊握著哈克夫人的雙手，將她的手臂高舉在頭上；而他的右手抓著她的脖子後方，迫使她面朝下地抵在他的胸口前。她白色的睡袍沾染了鮮血，一道細細的血絲，從他撕開的襯衫中裸露出的胸腔流下來。

當這群人衝進房裡時，伯爵轉過臉來，臉上突現兇惡的表情。他眼睛帶著惡魔般的憤怒，閃著紅色的光芒。他猛烈地將他的受害者丟回床上，轉過身來跳向那群追捕者面前。

就在此時，教授用一隻手牢牢地舉起十字架，吟誦了一段禱告詞，伯爵突然打住，就像可憐的露西當時在她的墳墓外一樣。接著伯爵向後退了回去。

p. 102–103 「哈，你還以為你已經擊敗我了呢。你可知道我不只已經活了好幾世紀了，我還會活到你的骨頭都變成塵土。現在你所愛的女人就要變成我的了！」他大叫著。

說完，他就消逝在夜晚的黑暗之中。

「我們必須比當初看顧露西時，還要更小心地看顧她。」凡‧赫辛說。

「明天我們就回去卡費斯，把伯爵最後一個箱子給摧毀掉。」

隔天上午吃早餐時，氣氛很奇怪。他們想振作精神，為彼此打氣，而米娜卻是當中最開朗、心情最好的。

用完餐後，凡‧赫辛站起來說：「現在，我親愛的朋友們，讓我們前去完成這個可怕的任務吧。大家都做好了像我們第一次造訪敵人巢穴那晚的武裝準備了嗎？」

大家都向他確信已做好準備。「那就好。現在，米娜小姐，不管怎樣，在太陽下山前妳都會很安全。但是我們離開前，我來幫妳做好妳個人的防備。從妳下樓之後，我就已經在妳的房間放好大蒜、聖水和聖餅了。這樣一來，他應該不會進去了。現在讓我幫妳做好防備。我以天父天子的聖名，以這塊聖餅碰觸妳的額頭……」

當他一把聖餅放在她的額頭上，米娜就發出了可怕的尖叫聲。那塊薄薄的聖餅烙進了她的肉裡，就好像一塊白熱的鑄鐵。

p. 104–105 凡‧赫辛看來很沮喪。

「親愛的米娜，請原諒我。」他說。

他神情堅定轉身面向其他人說：「趁陽光還照耀時，我們去消滅那個怪物的最後藏身之處吧。」

強納生留下來看顧米娜，其他人都回到了卡費斯，但他們卻找不到那個最後的箱子。

回到米娜的房間後，凡‧赫辛說：「既然米娜喝過了伯爵的血了，那她現在和他之間就產生了一種特殊的連結。她可以接收到伯爵現在所經歷的一切，反之亦然。」

凡‧赫辛將米娜催眠。「妳看到了什麼？」他問：「妳聽到什麼？聞到了什麼？」

米娜雙眼緊閉著，緩慢地說：「一切又暗又悶，就像在箱子裡一樣。我可以聞到海的味道，聽到浪潮的聲音，還有一艘船準備出航。」

「那就是了，他要回去外西凡尼亞了，我們已經成功地把他趕出倫敦了！」強納生大叫。

「是，沒錯。」凡‧赫辛答道：「但是為了米娜好，我們要去追蹤他，摧毀他。如果動作太慢，米娜就會走上和露西一樣的命運。」

於是他們決定了，凡‧赫辛和米娜一起從陸路到德古拉的城堡；而強納生、史華德醫師和亞瑟則搭上快船，從海上走水路追剿德古拉。凡‧赫辛和米娜平安地早一步在伯爵和其他人之前抵達城堡。

天氣非常寒冷，凡‧赫辛很擔心米娜的狀況。米娜在夜裡無法入眠，會進入一種恍神狀態；白天則睡得很沉，沉到凡‧赫辛根本叫不醒她。只有在日出與日落的短暫時刻，她才能正常的活動。

p. 106–107 這是米娜寫在她日記裡的內容：

下午四五點，我醒來了。教授向我示意，我起身跟著他。他找到了一個絕佳點，一個自然形成的岩石孔洞，在兩個大圓石中間有個像是門的入口。他牽著我的手，拉我進去。

他說：「妳看！妳可以躲在這裡，要是野狼來了，我也可以一次應付一隻。」

他把我們的毛皮拿進來，幫我鋪了個舒適的小窩，還試著拿一些食物給我，但食物一靠近嘴邊我就會作噁。我想要討他高興，但我就是無法叫自己吃下去。他看起來很難過，卻沒有責備我。他把望遠鏡從盒裡拿出來，站在岩石頂上開始搜尋地平線。

突然他大叫：「看！米娜小姐！妳看！妳看！」

我跳起來站在他身邊的石頭上。他把望遠鏡給我，指給我看。雪下更大了，一陣強風吹得雪花猛烈地打旋。從我們所在的高度可看到遠方。

p. 108–109 就在我們前方不遠處，有一群騎士匆匆地騎過來。他們中間是一輛長長的運貨馬車，馬車左右來回搖擺著，就像晃來晃去的狗尾巴一樣。從那些人的服裝，我可以認出他們是一些鄉下人或是吉普賽人之類的。

馬車上有一個大大的方形箱子。我一看到，心臟就快跳出來了，因為我知道一切就快結束了。夜晚即將降臨，而我知道，日落時箱子裡的那玩意兒就自由了。

我害怕地轉向教授，但是出人意料的是他並不在那裡。不一會兒，我看到他在我的下方。他在我站的位置上畫了一個神聖的圓圈，並用禱詞加封。

完事後，他站到我身邊告訴我：「至少在這兒妳就可以安全不受他的威脅了。」

他拿回我的望遠鏡，說：「妳看，他們來得真快，他們正鞭打馬匹盡速飛駛。」

他停了一下，然後用低沉的聲音說：「他們正在和日落賽跑，我們可能會太慢了。」

然後他大叫著：「看！看！看！有兩個騎馬的人從南方快速跟上來了，那鐵定是亞瑟和約翰！」

我拿起望遠鏡看，這兩人可能是史華德醫師和霍伍德先生。

p. 110–111 無論如何，我知道他們兩人都不是強納生。但不知為什麼，我知道強納生就在不遠處。我環顧四周，看到在北方有另外兩人飛速騎馬前來。我知道其中一人是強納生，另一個是戈達明先生，他是亞瑟在倫敦的朋友，滿懷熱心地加入我們危險的追捕行動。他們也在追趕拉著貨車的那群人。

我告訴教授，他像個小男孩般高興地大叫。然後他靠著岩石，把他的溫徹斯特步槍準備好。

「大家全都聚集過來了。」他說：「當時間一到，吉普賽人就會從四面八方被包圍了。」

我拿出我的左輪手槍。我們在說話的當下，狼嚎聲逐漸逼近，狼群也聚集起來準備要覓食。

等待的每一刻就像一年那麼長。此時風激烈地呼嘯著，雪花也猛吹狂打，但是陽光卻仍照耀著四周。我們已經習慣等待日出日落，所以我們很確切地知道太陽就快下山了。

p. 112–113 不久，我們就能夠很清楚地分辨出伯爵與我們、獵人和獵物兩方的人馬。奇怪的是，那些吉普賽人似乎沒有察覺，或根本不在乎有人在追趕。太陽在山頭上愈沉愈低，他們也好像加倍了速度。

突然間，兩個聲音大喊：「停下來！」。

一個我們是強納生，另一個則是霍伍德先生果決權威的命令。吉普賽人或許聽不懂語言，但卻沒有會錯我們的意。他們出於本能地將馬拉緊停住。

戈達明先生和強納生衝到一邊，而史華德醫師與霍伍德先生走到另一頭。吉普賽頭頭揮手要他們後退，並厲聲告訴夥伴繼續前進。

他們鞭策馬向前，但這四人舉起溫徹斯特式來福槍，這時凡・赫辛醫師和我走出石頭，用武器瞄準他們。吉普賽人看到自己被包圍便聚攏一起，他們的頭頭轉向他們說了一些話，命每人拿起手上的刀槍等各式武器，做好準備攻擊的姿勢。

p. 114–115 那吉普賽頭頭先指著即將沉入山頭的夕陽，又指著城堡。他說了一些我聽不懂的話。猶如在回應他的話一般，我們這方四人全下馬衝向貨車。

奇怪的是，我並不害怕，只是有種狂野欲望想有所行動。看到我們這方人行動快速，吉普賽頭頭下了一道命令，他的人迅速把貨車圍成一個圓圈。

我看到強納生在人牆的一邊，而亞瑟在另一邊，兩人正努力地推進到貨車旁。很明顯地，他們已決心要在日落前達成任務，沒有任何東西可以加以阻撓。

不管是前方瞄準的武器，還是吉普賽人白亮的刀子，或是背後狼群的咆哮，看來似乎都無法分散他們的注意力。強納生堅決的表情和對目標的專注，似乎嚇阻了他面前的吉普賽人。

吉普賽人本能地退縮一旁，讓他通過。就在那一瞬間，他跳上貨車，用一種不可思議的力量，將那個大箱子推過邊緣掉到地上。

p. 116–117 這時，亞瑟也不顧一切地往前衝，而吉普賽人卻用閃亮的刀子向他猛擊，他操著大波伊刀擋開攻擊。一開始，我以為他挺過了，但當他現身在貨車上跳下來的強納生身旁時，我看到他左手抓著身體的一側，血從指間噴出來。

　　但他並沒有誤事，亞瑟和強納生的行動讓箱蓋開始鬆動，釘子被拔出來，發出尖銳刺耳聲音，箱蓋板也被丟回去。

　　就在這時，那些發現自己被戈達明先生、史華德醫師和凡·赫辛的來福槍包圍的吉普賽人決定讓步，不再做進一步的抵抗。

　　太陽就快沉下山頭，我看到伯爵躺在箱子裡，一片死白，紅眼怒瞪著，流露出我熟悉的可怕憎恨。我看著他，他的眼睛一看到沉沒的夕陽，眼神中的憎恨就轉成了勝利的喜悅。

　　但是剎那間強納生揮舞閃亮的大刀，我看到他砍破伯爵的喉嚨時，尖叫出聲。而就在同時，亞瑟的波伊刀刺進他的心臟。

p. 118–119 彷彿奇蹟般，我們親眼看到他整個軀體化作塵土消失眼前。我很慶幸我能活著見證，在那一刻，德古拉的臉上一片祥和，我從沒想像過這樣的表情會出現在他臉上。

那些吉普賽人調了頭，一句話也沒留，逃命似地騎著馬走了。而那些走路的人跳上貨車，大喊要馬夫別遺棄他們。狼群也跟在他們後面離開，留下我們一行人。

亞瑟靠著手肘攤倒在地上，手壓住身體一側，鮮血仍從指間湧出。我跑向他，兩位醫生也跑過去，強納生跪在他身後，亞瑟嘆了口氣，衰弱地將我的手握進他未染血的手中。

他一定是從我臉上看到了我內心的痛苦，因為他微笑著對我說：「我只是很高興自己能幫上忙。喔！天啊！」他突然大叫掙扎著想坐起來，指著我：「我死也值得了！看啊！妳看！」

夕陽現在正落在山巔上，紅色微光照在我臉龐，彷如沐浴在玫瑰色光芒中。就在這瞬間，所有人激動地跪了下來，嘴裡都喊了一聲深切誠摯的「阿門」，因為他們看到那烙印在我額上的紅色印記竟然消失了！

亞瑟說：「現在我們該感謝上帝，一切都沒有白費。你們看，詛咒已經消失了。」

在我們痛苦的悲傷中，這位英勇的紳士帶著微笑，在沉靜中辭世了。

Answers

P. 56   **A** ❶ ❹ ❻

       B ❶ Slovaks   ❷ Gypsies   ❸ Three women

       C ❶ F   ❷ T   ❸ T   ❹ F   ❺ F

P. 57   **D** ❶ (b)   ❷ (c)   ❸ (a)

       E ❷ → ❺ → ❶ → ❸ → ❹

P. 86   **A** ❶ spirits   ❷ heartbeat   ❸ ignorance
           ❹ bare

       B ❶ (d)   ❷ (b)   ❸ (c)   ❹ (a)

P. 87   **C** ❶ F   ❷ T   ❸ F   ❹ T

       D ❶ (b)   ❷ (a)

P. 120   **A** ❶ T   ❷ F   ❸ T   ❹ F   ❺ T   ❻ F

       B ❶ → ❹ → ❷ → ❺ → ❸

P. 121   **C** ❶ (b)   ❷ (c)   ❸ (a)   ❹ (b)

P. 132 **A** **1** This person knew a lot about the weaknesses of vampires. (Van Helsing)

2 This person died and became a vampire in England. (Lucy)

3 This person sailed to England on a Russian ship. (Count Dracula)

4 This person was almost killed by three female vampires. (Jonathan)

5 This person lost both a lover and a father. (Arthur Holmwood)

B **1** asked, about   **2** wiped, eyes
3 excellent, intonation   **4** arrives, leave
5 take, toll

P. 133 **C** **1** Who helped Dracula prepare for his move to London? (b)

2 Where did Mina find Jonathan in the hospital? (c)

D **1** Count Dracula's home is in Monrovia. (F)
2 Jonathan is engaged to marry Mina. (T)
3 Dr. Seward was a former student of Dr. Van Helsing. (T)
4 Arthur put a wooden stake through Lucy's heart. (T)

吸血鬼【二版】
Dracula

作者 _ 伯蘭・史杜克
　　　（Bram Stoker）

改寫 _ Brian J. Stuart

插圖 _ Julina Alekcangra

翻譯 _ 林育珊

編輯 _ 歐寶妮

作者 / 故事簡介翻譯 _ 王采翎

校對 _ 張盛傑

封面設計 _ 林書玉

排版 _ 葳豐 / 林書玉

製程管理 _ 洪巧玲

發行人 _ 周均亮

出版者 _ 寂天文化事業股份有限公司

電話 _ +886-2-2365-9739

傳真 _ +886-2-2365-9835

網址 _ www.icosmos.com.tw

讀者服務 _ onlineservice@icosmos.com.tw

出版日期 _ 2020年1月 二版一刷（250201）

郵撥帳號 _ 1998620-0 寂天文化事業股份有限公司

國家圖書館出版品預行編目資料

吸血鬼 / Bram Stoker 原著；Brian J. Stuart 改寫 . --
二版 . -- [臺北市]：寂天文化，2020.01
　　面；　公分 . -- (Grade 5 經典文學讀本)
　譯自：Dracula
　ISBN 978-986-318-878-0(25K 平裝附光碟片)

　1. 英語 2. 讀本

　　　　805.18　　108022348